A Shepherd Security Christmas

Shepherd Security Book #14.5

Margaret Kay

Sisters Romance

Shepherd Security Organizational Chart

Classified: Top Secret

Colonel Samuel 'Big Bear' Shepherd,
Retired US Army

Alpha Team
John 'Coop' Cooper
Alexander 'Doc' Williams
Anthony 'Razor' Garcia
Ethan 'Jax' Jackson
Madison 'Xena' Miller

Delta Team
Landon 'Lambchop' Johnson
Danny 'Mother' Trio
Gary 'the Undertaker' Sloan
Brian 'the Birdman' Sherman

Charlie Team
Jimmy 'Taco' Wilson
Mike 'Powder' Rogers
Rich 'Handsome' Burke
Carter 'Moe' Tessman

Bravo Team
Tommy 'Louisa' Flores
Eddie 'Needles' Winston
Kenny 'Ducky' Gallup

Elijah 'Kegger' Robinson

Echo Team
Brody 'BT' Templeton
Michael 'Bubbles' Cooper
Sebastian 'Crash' Roth
Laura Lee 'Lah-lee' Saxton

Operations Center Analysts
Yvette 'Control' Donaldson
Anthony 'Wang' Miraldi
Caleb 'Hound dog' Smith
Brad 'Circles' Dupont

Other Agency Staff
Angel Jackson – Office Manager
Michaela Karras – TechLab Manager
Elizabeth Williams – Receptionist (PT)
Dahlia Jarboe – Receptionist (PT)
Brielle Jarboe-Sherman – Special Projects Manager
Requisition Ryan Grant – Supply Chain Manager
Dr. Joe Lassiter – Team Mental Health Professional

The Holiday's Through Angel's Eyes

I was asked recently, what are my Holiday Traditions? My answer was, wow, that is a question that spans all of my roles. I am the Shepherd Security Office Manager, Executive Assistant to Shepherd, the wife of one of the Operators, and a mother. I kind of feel like, in a way, I am the wife or the mother to all the Operators, even those who are now married. I take care of them all. I make sure the holidays are celebrated well and often remind Shepherd that his people need a break to come together as the family they are during the holiday season. He's focused on operations, I get that, but his people are human.

Before I became a part of Shepherd Security, anyone who wasn't active on a mission celebrated Christmas by putting up a Christmas Tree, having a meal together, and a Christmas Eve sermon performed by the team pastor, Landon 'Lambchop' Johnson, if he was in town. The entire celebration lasted a couple of hours. Shepherd Security is a twenty-four-hour, seven day a week operation that does important work. Christmas was merely a blip on their radar.

The Christmas celebration has bloomed into so much more than it was, with Christmas Eve being the day we all celebrate together. The comradery is something I'd never experienced growing up, the only child of a single mother. My husband tells me our celebrations now are more like what active-duty units deployed away from their family's experience. We all hang out, sing Christmas carols, watch Christmas movies, play board games, laugh, and share what our favorite Christmas memories are from our childhoods. It's like we are snowed in at a ski lodge. And we keep the birth of Jesus at the center of the holiday. Lambchop makes sure of that!

The past few years, Shepherd has adjusted operations so that everyone on the team has a few days off between Christmas and New Year's Day, to partake of our office celebration on Christmas Eve and to travel to see family if they want. We're a tight group, a family. That's what I like the most. We're a big, loud, boisterous family!

I think that is at the heart of the holiday traditions we celebrate. Family doesn't have to be about blood relations. It's about who you care about, about spending time with those who are important to you. These teams spend so much time together. They risk their lives together. It's only natural that they would want to celebrate the holidays together, too.

After I joined the team, I felt it was important to give the guys a home-cooked meal and to really decorate the office well. I put up the decorations on December first, and we enjoy them for the entire month! I also make sure that all the employees have a gift. Shepherd pays for them, and I love to go shopping and pick out something I think each person will really cherish. I like the fact that Shepherd respects my opinion and ideas. We're a team.

After my baby, Sammy, was born, Shepherd didn't like the idea of me having to cook, so he began to cater a big dinner in. Together, he and I decide on the menu, and I take care of all the arrangements. I still make a bunch of sweet treats! Sammy's first Christmas was incredible. Everyone made the holiday about celebrating his first Christmas. Before he started preschool, he came to work with me every day, so Sammy is, in a way, everyone's baby. Even the toughest of the guys cradled him in their arms and doted on him. The same holds true now with Johanna, my six-month-old, who comes to work with me more than half of the week.

Several of the guys are now married or in long-term committed relationships, including Shepherd. His wedding was just a few months ago. His wife is a total sweetheart! I'm close to her and all the other women who have joined our ranks. I feel like they are all the sisters I never had. I bring them into the planning for the holidays now too.

Our Shepherd Security family has expanded

with four other children, brought into our lives. The children spend a lot of time together. They're being brought up as cousins. There are several new babies besides Johanna, who will celebrate their first Christmas this year. It will be a special year indeed!

I hope as my children grow up, they will feel what it's like to be part of this big family and appreciate it as much as I do. Being a part of Shepherd Security is a privilege, a wonderful privilege I am grateful for, especially during the holiday season!

A Shepherd Security Poem

Twas the night before Christmas, when all through HQ
Not a creature was stirring, not even you know who.
The assault rifles were hung in the
team lockers with care,
In hopes that all remained quiet, but
say it aloud they don't dare.
***

The Operators were nestled all snug in their beds,
With loved ones beside them, but nearby
their handguns and creds.
While Angel nursed Johanna,
Jackson and Sammy slept,
In a different bedroom across town, a
secret Sloan and Kaylee kept.
***

When out on the lawn there arose such a clatter,
Cooper and Madison sprang from their
bed to see what was the matter.
Armed with handguns they flew like a flash,
Confronting the intruder whose car it did crash.
***

The moon on the breast of the new-fallen snow,
Gave Lambchop and Michaela a clear glimpse below.
A late-night accident, the driver drunk but okay,
Cooper and Madison merely sent him
on his merry little way.
Hahna slept through it, feelings of safety
and love tucked her in tight,
Her past a distant memory, her dreams
sweet with no fright.
***

When what to Doc and Elizabeth's eyes should appear,
But their tiny little girl, drawing near.

7

She'd climbed out of her crib, with
a mischievous smile,
Anxious to snuggle, in her unique little style.
***

More rapid than eagles, Garcia did react,
He calmed Little T, with patience and tact.
Sienna, she smiled, loving her two favorite men,
With plans for another, perhaps named Carmen.
***

The Birdman and Brielle, slept cradling their baby boy,
While Annaka and Mother, birth
control they did employ.
Michael and Dahlia lay holding each other,
And neither one knew that Dahlia
would soon be a mother.
***

BT and Evie slept with Ollie at their feet,
But she snuck up between them, which
with her size was a miraculous feat.
And Smith and Hollyn, their first Christmas together,
Their love, it was strong, the storm it could weather.
***

Laura Lee and Dupont, best friends who'd say I do,
Snuggled asleep in his bed, they dreamed
Christmas dreams too.
Sebastian Roth in the middle of a lifechanging case,
The woman who's righteous, but
who has fallen from grace.
***

Doc Lassiter and his family, only
him we have so far met,
Had no way of knowing the dire plans
in motion that were set.
Rich Burke, whose story, we've only begun,
Will develop like a wildfire, as hot as the sun.
***

Jimmy Wilson, a woman, he met on a case,
Will call him with trouble, he'll respond to post-haste.
Tessman, the tough one, a Marine to the core,
A woman he's only dreamt of, his help she'll implore.
***

And Mike Rogers, dear Powder, he will
be challenged the most,
With a woman who's broken, or as
the guys say, is toast.
But fear not, gentle reader, Margaret Kay will prevail,
Powder and the woman their fates will
bounce back from the gale.
***

The four men of Bravo Team who we'll meet very soon,
All sexy, over 40, and they make the women swoon.
Tommy, Eddie, Kenny, and Elijah are their names,
You'll love them, I'm sure, as with
women they play no games.
***

Miraldi and Yvette, keeping watch at HQ,
They love every single member of the
Shepherd Security crew.
Requisition Ryan Grant his story we don't know,
He manages all supplies so that they never run low.
***

Shepherd and Diana, Big Bear and the beauty,
Our big boss is awake, as he's always on duty.
Tonight though he'll rest, because
all in the world it is right,
And before he drifts off, he utters "Happy
Christmas to all, and to all a good night!"

Alpha

December 2nd Saturday

Angel hoisted baby Johanna onto her hip. At six months old, she was a happy, friendly baby who slept great and was a healthy thirteen pounds. She had black hair and hazel green eyes, just like her big brother, Sammy. Angel stood behind her desk at the Shepherd Security office. Johanna came to work with her two to three days a week. She worked from home one to two days a week, and the rest of the time, Elizabeth Williams watched the baby with the other children of the Shepherd Security personnel who were not in school.

Angel's son, Sammy was in a three morning a week preschool program at a preschool near their home. Elizabeth watched him those afternoons and one full day each week and he was home with Angel and Johanna the other day each week. It was the perfect schedule as far as Angel was concerned. He got to have time at school with other children his age, he had time at Elizabeth's with the other Shepherd Security children, and he had one weekday a week at home with his mom and sister, plus all weekend.

Elizabeth was amazing with the kids. Her daughter, Olivia, was a year and a half old, but she still managed to watch not only Angel's kids, but also Anthony 'Razor' Garcia and Sienna's nine-month-old son Little T, and Bastian, who was Brielle and Brian 'the Birdman' Sherman's five-month-old son. She only watched him part-time though when Brielle was in the office, which usually lined up with Sammy's preschool days. Shepherd had granted Brielle a liberal work from home schedule.

Oh, and Elizabeth also watched Hahna, the tiny five-year-old adopted daughter of John 'Coop' Cooper and Madison 'Xena' Miller, when she was not in the five day a week, full day Pre-K program at the preschool. Hahna also had a bedroom at Elizabeth and Alexander 'Doc' Williams' house, and she stayed with them when Madison and Cooper were working. They were her second parents.

Today was Saturday though, so Elizabeth was not babysitting anyone. Sammy was at home with his daddy, the man who Angel loved with all her heart, Ethan 'Jax' Jackson. He had saved her life and filled her heart and life with more joy than she thought one person could experience.

Sam 'Big Bear' Shepherd was in his office working, because he basically worked every day of the week except for Sunday afternoons. His wife, Diana, insisted on one afternoon off a week and unless there was something major going down, Shepherd took off Sunday afternoons to spend with his bride of a few months.

Cooper came through the hallway from the direction of the rec room and his office. "Hey, Lambchop, Mother, and I have gotten all the boxes you needed in the rec room, and we moved the furniture as you requested. I'm due for a meeting with Shepherd, but Lambchop and Mother will stay and help you unbox everything and then haul the empty boxes back to storage. Madison's bringing Hahna in with her to decorate. Hahna is so excited to see the Christmas Tree this year."

"I think she's more excited about the presents," Angel said with a laugh. "But I know this year is different for her now that she's been here for a whole year. I know she was still traumatized and didn't fully understand what Christmas was about last year."

Coop smiled a big, proud, fatherly grin. "Yeah, this year will be fun. She sure understands Santa Claus this year."

Angel laughed more. "It doesn't take them long to understand Santa means gifts."

"I'll catch you later," Cooper said. He passed her desk and continued down the hallway towards

Shepherd's office.

Once he was inside with the door closed, the private, interior elevator door opened. Kaylee Sloan, Brielle Sherman, and Michaela Karas spilled into the hall, laughing, and chatting loudly. Angel greeted them warmly. Kaylee took JoJo, as she called her, from Angel's arms and hugged her, showering her with kisses. Kaylee was Gary 'the Undertaker' Sloan's wife. They'd been trying to have a child since they'd gotten married. Kaylee had suffered a miscarriage earlier in the year and Angel knew it had been hard for her to watch her friends get pregnant and have babies of their own. But that hadn't stopped her from sharing in her friends' excitement and giving their babies a lot of love.

Michaela was five months pregnant with her and Landon 'Lambchop' Johnson's child. Much to his chagrin, they weren't married yet. Their wedding was scheduled to take place on New Year's Eve. Angel prayed nothing big would go down anywhere that would scramble the teams and interrupt their wedding. In this business, you just couldn't count on anything, unless Shepherd removed the team from standby, which he rarely did.

All three women had worked for Shepherd Security. Brielle was a member of the Digital Team, Michaela was the inventor extraordinaire of the team's gadgets, and Kaylee, though a music teacher at a local elementary school during the school year, had worked as Angel's backup over the summer while she was on maternity leave.

Before the women could head down the hall to the rec room, Elizabeth, Madison, and Hahna came walking through the interior hallway, having just come up the stairs from the parking garage. Hahna ran ahead of the two women greeting all her 'aunts' with hugs, her excitement on full display.

Once in the large rec room, the women got busy. The men had put the Christmas Tree together and removed the large box it was stored in. Tubs containing ornaments and other decorations were stacked near it. The tree always resided in the same spot, centered against the far wall. In the foreground, tables and chairs would be arranged for the Christmas Eve feast for forty-five to fifty people.

Kaylee set the baby in a bouncy chair that Angel had in the room and then she and Brielle tacked the lit garland around the door to Cooper's office. "Where are you going to order dinner from this year?"

"That's a secret," Angel said with a mysterious smile. "But it's going to be delicious!"

"It always is," Madison said. "Wasn't Sienna

going to come help today?"

"She isn't going to make it," Angel said. "Little T is cutting some teeth and he had her awake all night. She was going to try to lie down while he takes his afternoon nap."

"Garcia's in Ops, isn't he?" Michaela asked.

"Yes," Angel said. "Jackson was going to watch Little T while she was here, but she wanted to spare him misery with a cranky baby."

"It's so nice to have the guys home for a few days," Kaylee said.

"Shh," the others hushed her in unison.

"You know you just jinxed it. Now they're going to get scrambled," Brielle said.

"Saying it doesn't jinx it," Kaylee argued as she unboxed ornaments.

"Kaylee's right," Madison said. "I don't believe in any of that superstitious nonsense."

"What's supser-tichous mean, mommy?" Hahna asked.

"Superstitious, honey. And it's believing something will happen because you talk about it, like it will bring bad luck. Things just happen. Nothing people do cause them to happen," she told her. Then she handed Hahna another ornament to put on the tree.

Lambchop and Danny 'Mother' Trio walked back into the room. Lambchop greeted everyone and then embraced Michaela. "How are my girls?" He had his hand on her baby bump.

"Girls?" Angel asked. "Did you find out the gender and not tell anyone?"

"We just did," Lambchop said with a grin.

"We had another sonogram yesterday at the OB and it was clear that it's a girl." Her smile was as big as Lambchop's.

The others all congratulated them. Mother just smiled. He already knew.

With all the hands working on the decorations, they soon had the room transformed into a Christmas wonderland.

Bravo

On Monday morning Angel arrived at the office just after nine-thirty. She'd left Johanna with Elizabeth and driven Sammy and Hahna to school. She had financial spreadsheets to prepare, to close out November for Shepherd. She couldn't afford to be distracted by Johanna. Jackson had left before six. All five members of Alpha Team plus Echo Team member Sebastian 'Crash' Roth had deployed on the next CIA Referral Case. Roth was to be assigned to HQ for traditional cases for another two weeks. He hoped to get in two more missions before rotating back to the PGP Install project. He'd already completed one the previous week, though from what Roth had said, he didn't consider it completed.

Also from Echo Team, Laura Lee 'Lah-lee' Saxton was still assigned to HQ. She was receiving full Operator Training. Several of the team members would be providing her with different aspects of that training. This week, Lambchop would be at HQ covering firearms, ammunition, and also training in explosives. They would both also provide backup coverage in Ops.

The remainder of Echo Team, Brody 'BT' Templeton and Michael 'Bubbles' Cooper had left with the three remaining members of Delta Team, Mother, Sloan, and Sherman, plus Jimmy 'Taco' Wilson from Charlie Team for the next DEA Partner Mission. BT and Wilson would co-lead the team, a first. It was deemed a low-risk mission.

The last three members of Charlie Team, Mike 'Powder' Rogers, Carter 'Moe' Tessman, and Rich 'Handsome' Burke departed at seven this morning for their next PGP Install in Wisconsin. They drove one of the agency's SUVs as it was so close, and the agency Lear was in use shuttling the team consisting of mostly Delta and Echo team members to their destination, which was Memphis, Tennessee.

Angel sighed; it would be quiet around the office with everyone deployed this week. She and the two other Alpha Team wives, Sienna and Elizabeth already had plans to get together for dinner at her house that evening. They usually did a few nights during the week when the team was deployed. She knew that the Delta Team wives and girlfriends did when their men were deployed as well.

Her phone chirped a text message from Shepherd. Upon arriving, she'd logged herself as in on the staff calendar, so he knew she was there.

She checked the display. As expected, Shepherd wanted her to come to his office.

She grabbed her notebook from the desk and walked the short distance down the hallway to his office. The door was open when she arrived and she was surprised to find Shepherd's wife, Diana, there. She had a chiropractic and physical therapy clinic on the second floor of the building. "Good morning to you both," Angel said with a smile.

Diana stepped to her as she walked further into the office and gave her an embrace in greeting. "Hi, Angel. The rec room looks great. You ladies did a wonderful job. I'm sorry I was busy and couldn't help."

"I'm sorry we couldn't do it Sunday morning when you were available," Angel said. Then her attention turned to Shepherd. "I'll be working on those spreadsheets this morning. What else do you need me to take care of?"

"Not urgent, but when you can, the four members of Bravo Team are due to check in by December twenty-second. Can you get them each a room at the Extended Stay down the road? Book it through January thirtieth."

"Them each a room?" Angel asked. Normally, the Operators shared rooms on missions.

"Yes, they'll be working different hours

training, so them each having their own space will be appreciated by them, I'm sure."

Angel noted it in her book. "I'll get it taken care of today." She smiled and waited to see if he had anything else.

"Thank you," Shepherd said. "I also wanted to talk to you about the Christmas gifts for each employee this year, as I know you start early. I also want to include gifts for each of the children, which Diana will take care of."

Diana smiled and nodded. "Well, the gifts for the children will technically be from Sam and me, but I wanted you to know so that you didn't get them something from the agency too as the card will be signed Shepherd Security."

"But just like last year, I'd like the gift from the agency to each couple to be something for them both. You did a great job last year, not sure you can top it this year," Shepherd said.

"Challenge accepted," Angel said with a grin.

Shepherd and Diana laughed. "Same budget for each this year."

"That's very generous of you," Angel said.

"The men work hard and are gone a lot, laying their lives on the line. Their wives or girlfriends put up with a lot. They deserve it," Shepherd acknowledged.

Diana embraced him. "Yes, we do."

"And I also wanted to let you know that with Michaela and Lambchop's wedding scheduled for New Year's Eve, I'll be shifting the leave rotation from prior years to accommodate it. I'm pulling the team from emergency standby with the DoD December twenty-fourth through January first."

Angel was shocked he was doing so. He'd pulled them from standby for three days over his wedding just a few months previously. This was only the second time since she'd been a part of Shepherd Security that he was doing it. Her gaze went to Diana, who smiled like the instigator of a coup.

"Each member of the team will get five days of leave from December twenty-fifth through December thirtieth, everyone due back December thirty-first for the wedding," Shepherd continued. Lambchop will be staffed to cover Ops with Yvette and Miraldi during that time. Yvette and Miraldi will gladly take their leave time in January and of course Lambchop and Michaela will take their honeymoon the first week of January. I spoke with Cooper, Jax, and Garcia this morning. They each agreed to take a couple of shifts in Ops over their leave as they all indicated they are not traveling for the holiday. I'll owe them a few days off in January to comp them," Shepherd said.

Angel was surprised to hear that Cooper

and Madison weren't traveling to Arizona to be with her parents this year. She'd have to talk with Madison about that when she got the chance. She already knew that Garcia and Sienna would not be traveling, and it came as no surprise that Garcia had volunteered to take a few shifts. Even if he wasn't scheduled, he would be in. And she didn't mind that Jackson had also volunteered. He and Garcia were, after all, number three and four in charge of the agency with full decision-making power.

"I'm sure everyone will be surprised and happy with the leave schedule," Angel said.

"I plan to send an email with the info out later today to everyone," Shepherd said.

Angel appreciated how he always told her things first when he could. "Anything else, boss?"

"No, thank you, Angel. And I agree with Diana. You ladies did a great job as always with the rec room."

Angel smiled and then left his office. She sat at her desk and got to work on the spreadsheets. Shepherd closely monitored all expenses and revenues. Her routine on the first business day of each new month included reconciling ten different spreadsheets and preparing monthly financial reports. She loved all aspects of her job and counted herself lucky to be a part of the team.

They'd literally saved her life, but she thanked God every day for the incredible life she had since that horrible time.

Diana left Sam's office and took the route that would lead her past Angel's desk. "Hey, I wanted to be sure you're okay with me taking over buying the gifts for the children this year," she said as she reached Angel. "I don't want to step on any toes."

Angel beamed her a thankful grin. "No toe stepping at all, so don't worry about that. And thank you. I do think though that you should sign the card from the two of you. I have a list of ideas. If you like, I can send it to you."

"I'd appreciate it if you do, thanks," Diana said. "You handle everything around here so well, I'm just glad I can help in some small way."

"I appreciate that you want to. Diana don't ever worry about stepping on my toes. If I've learned anything from the guys, it's that to accomplish any job quicker and to a higher standard it's best if we all pull together and do what we can. No egos are allowed in the mix."

"Thanks," Diana said. Then she hurried from the office. Her next patient was waiting.

Charlie

The agency Lear, en route to Memphis, Tennessee was at its cruising altitude. The six team members on board used this time to acquaint themselves with the target of the case, Germain Perez. In addition to owning two thriving hotels, the first in Memphis and the second across the river in West Memphis, Arkansas, he was suspected of being the head of the biggest fentanyl and heroin distribution network in Memphis. The problem was the authorities had no evidence to prove it. Even when a few low-level members of his crew flipped, it was merely hearsay. There was nothing to link Perez to the drugs, violence, or money. No judge would grant a warrant to surveil Perez.

Delta-Echo Team's mission was surveillance of Perez with the end goal of finding something that would enable the local police and DEA to get a warrant to conduct either official surveillance or a legal search. It was deemed low risk as there was to be no direct contact between the team and the target or any of the known drug runners or pushers.

Two things of interest in the material the local DEA and the Shepherd Security Digital Team had provided was that a low-level thug had provided information on one of Perez's drivers. He was an ex-con who went by the name Skits, real name Tomas Salazar, who served time for illegal gun trafficking and extortion. The second interesting item was that the second hotel Perez owned in West Memphis, Arkansas was a casino. And he kept a residence in the penthouse of the hotel portion even though his legal residence was the penthouse of the hotel in Memphis.

***

In the agency SUV, driving north towards the Alliant Energy Dam in Prairie du Sac on the Wisconsin River, northwest of Madison the three members of Charlie Team had nearly arrived. It was under a three-hour drive from HQ. The hydroelectric station provided electricity for over forty-five thousand people. If it were to be knocked out by hackers, it would have a substantial impact on the area. It wasn't a large operation, and the three members of the team were confident they could have the installation done in four days.

***

In two of the other agency vehicles, Alpha Team plus Roth drove northeast to New Buffalo,

Michigan, which was just over a three-hour drive as long as there was no lake effect snow coming off of Lake Michigan. This morning, they were lucky. It was clear but the stiff wind coming off the lake was frigid. The CIA referral case they would work this week also focused on a hotel and casino owner. Johnathan Burlington had just opened a resort casino along the New Buffalo coastline of Lake Michigan. The FBI were investigating the funding of the resort but the information the CIA stumbled across showed email content that was flagged with a foreign national in Dubai as it was in an unbreakable code. The Shepherd Security Team would conduct surveillance as well as poke around in the resort's operations to see if anything illegal jumped out.

***

That evening, Sienna brought Little T to Angel's home about an hour after she'd picked him up from Elizabeth's house. Elizabeth brought over Olivia and Hahna. Angel had put chicken in the crockpot before leaving for work. She was just finishing up the rest of the meal when the others arrived.

"Oh, my goodness, Angel!" Sienna exclaimed. "You already have your Christmas tree and all your decorations up. I don't know where you find the time to do all that you do."

Angel waved her off dismissively. "Jackson

and I put it all up the weekend after Thanksgiving. If we didn't then, I knew it would be weeks before I'd have time."

"It looks festive. You've inspired me. I think I'll start after I put Little T to bed tonight. I've structured my lessons so that I have no grading to do on Monday nights. I found it helps me start my work week with less stress and exhaustion."

"I couldn't believe the amount of grading you had when I stayed with you and helped," Elizabeth chimed in. "There has to be a way to lighten your workload. And I agree with Sienna, Angel. Your decorations look wonderful. When Alexander gets home, we're going to put ours up. I ordered the cutest felt tree for the kids. It adheres to the wall. The decorations stick to it so they can put them on and take them off all day long."

"I'm sure they'll have a lot of fun with that," Angel replied. "Jackson thinks they'll wrap up the case in a matter of days. They may make it home by Thursday." She glanced over at Hahna and Sammy playing across the room to be sure they were busy with their play before she spoke. It had come to a point where they needed to be careful what they said in front of the two oldest children as they understood more and would repeat what they heard.

"That would be nice," Elizabeth agreed in a whisper. "I like it when they do these CIA Referral cases much better than the DEA Partner Missions. I don't worry nearly as much about them."

"Anthony feels the same way," Sienna said quietly as she placed Little T in the highchair. "He told me the vibe on the team is much more relaxed with the CIA cases as opposed to the intense feel of the DEA cases. With the DEA cases they know there's going to be guns and violence. It just naturally comes with that much money exchanging hands."

"Yeah, those people have no regard for human life," Angel whispered. "They have no qualms about killing anyone." Then she raised her voice and called Sammy and Hahna over for dinner.

Angel had already prepared the kids' plates, so the food had time to cool. Once they were all sat at the table, the three women made their plates as well and joined them. All conversation regarding the team stopped and they talked with Hahna and Sammy about school that day and what they wanted for Christmas this year.

***

At Brian and Brielle Sherman's townhouse in a subdivision a few miles away, Brielle, Michaela, Kaylee, and Dahlia sat at Brielle's kitchen table. Her son, Bastian was taking a nap. One place setting was empty, waiting for Annaka,

Mother's fiancé to arrive. Her train from Chicago was running late. It was stopped on the tracks investigating a person who'd been struck by another train, usually a suicide. They weren't even near a station, as if they were, Annaka would have gotten off the train and gotten an Uber to get home.

"I don't care what anyone says," Brielle said. "There are no low-risk DEA missions." And she should know. She wrote articles under a fictitious name of any case the team was involved in to explain operations in a way that kept the Shepherd Security Team out of it. To write these articles, she viewed mission feed and read the mission prep reports as well as the Mission Reports upon the conclusion of each mission. She saw and knew a lot that the other women did not.

"Gary said they'll only be doing surveillance this time. No interaction with the buyers, sellers, or distributors," Kaylee said. "I know the work they do is important. Drugs are everywhere and its impact touches even kids in elementary school. One of our kids' older brother overdosed yesterday. His mother found him when she got home after work. It was too late to revive him." Kaylee was a music teacher at the same kindergarten through fifth grade school where Sienna taught.

"Oh, that poor kid," Dahlia said. "And that mom, I can't even imagine finding your own child dead."

Brielle shuddered. No, she couldn't either.

Dahlia reached over and took her sister's hand. "Sorry, you didn't need to think about that."

Brielle shook it off. "No, but it is hard not to think about Bastian when I hear something like that. Things hit you so differently after you have a baby."

Kaylee grasped her other hand. "Only when you're a phenomenal mother like you are."

"Thanks," Brielle said. "You will be too one day. I know you will."

Dahlia's gaze drifted across the table to Michaela. "And I know you're going to be an incredible mom too. And we all know Lambchop is going to be a great dad."

"Thanks," Michaela said, rubbing her baby bump. "She is going to be so lucky surrounded by all of you."

Just then, Annaka came through the front door. They all knew the lock codes to each other's places, and she saw the group of women sitting at the kitchen table as she approached the door. "Hi all, what a night!" Her gaze swept the table and saw that as she'd requested, they hadn't waited for her to eat. And she saw the open bottle of wine. "Oh, good. You have a bottle of wine open. I'm glad you didn't wait dinner on me."

"It's still warm, on the stove," Brielle said. "I'll pour you a glass as you get your plate."

"So, was it a person hit on the tracks?" Kaylee asked.

"Yes, they said it was. I was exhausted this morning and couldn't get going so I got a late start. I stayed a little later to make up the time, or I would have been on the train that hit the person. That poor conductor, knowing he was going to kill someone but unable to stop in time." She set her plate onto the table and took a seat. Brielle slid the glass of pinot over to her. "Thank you. I hope you all had a better day than I did."

"How are your whales?" Kaylee asked. She knew the belugas at the Shedd Aquarium were Annaka's babies. As far as she knew, Annaka and Mother weren't planning to have children even though it was obvious they'd both make amazing parents.

Annaka smiled fondly. "They're good, thriving. We had a group of seventh graders at the Shedd today and several of the kids asked what kind of education they needed to work with the whales like I do. I loved that they knew it would take advanced education and were thinking about their future careers."

All the ladies had gone to the Shedd

Aquarium as Annaka's guests behind the scenes and saw her in action with her whales. Her dedication to them was apparent to anyone who watched her. And her patience with the kids and her love of educating them when they visited the aquarium showed how good she was at her job.

"Michaela, isn't Lambchop home this week?" Kaylee asked, wondering why she was with them and not him.

"Yes, but he's working late at the office. He won't be home until after I'm in bed."

"That's right. He's training Laura Lee this week, isn't he?" Dahlia asked.

"Yes. He's glad she requested the additional training. And I'm glad he's home this week because of it," Michaela said with a laugh. "Oh, hey did you hear? Landon and I put an offer in yesterday on a house across the street from Madison and Cooper. It's a great four-bedroom house with an amazing back yard."

"Really, oh, that's great," the other ladies each replied, overlapping each other's words.

"We gave them two days to get back to us in the offer. I'm hoping to hear something tonight."

"I think Angel and Jackson were talking about moving over into that neighborhood at some point too. I know Angel wants a bigger yard for the kids to play in," Kaylee said.

"In a few years they do," Dahlia said. "Before Sammy is in kindergarten. Right now, she appreciates being so close to Elizabeth and Sienna."

"Yes, there is something to be said about living close to the team members," Kaylee agreed. "And I am so thankful we all live so close to each other. You know, not everyone is as lucky as we are to have this kind of family closeness with good friends." Tears gathered in her eyes.

"Kaylee, are you okay?" Dahlia asked.

"Yes, just feeling emotional today. I don't know why. My period is due, that must be it," Kaylee said.

"Well, thinking about that boy who lost his brother to an overdose isn't helping either," Dahlia said. "No more sad topics tonight."

***

In the penthouse apartment on the tenth floor of the Shepherd Security Building, Diana came through the door to find Sam in the kitchen. He'd made them salmon for dinner. She embraced him from behind. "I love how you cook for me on my late nights. Reminds me of those dinners we had when we first met."

Shepherd turned and wrapped his arms

around her, drawing her in for a kiss. "It's the least I can do for you on your late nights. And I loved those dinners too. I have a bottle of Pinot Gris in the refrigerator. Will you pour us both a glass?"

"You think of everything as usual." She opened the fridge and pulled out the chilled bottle. She noticed that he also had a spinach salad made. She appreciated him and his efforts knowing that she was the luckiest woman to have him in her life. Yes, his work hours were long, and agency business interfered with a lot of their plans, but she wouldn't have it any other way. Sam Shepherd was dedicated to the job at his core. It was who he was, and she loved the man he was.

Delta

In Memphis, the low-risk surveillance job went sideways on their second day on the ground. Sloan and BT went into the casino in West Memphis to look around after they'd observed Perez and his entourage enter. They quickly picked up on what was going on. They transmitted the obvious to the team. Perez was using his casino to launder the drug money. It was the perfect set up.

It was easy to spot his crew, even though they tried to act like normal gamblers. After Perez arrived at the casino, two men and two women strolled in behind him. Tomas 'Skits' Salazar was one of them. They headed directly to a blackjack table off to the side in a semi-private area that opened only as they arrived. Another couple and a solo man immediately joined them as did a female dealer.

The semi-private section they played in was one indication. Their high spirits while losing thousands, was another give away. The casino only records information on people who win for the IRS. They are supposed to record losses in excess of ten thousand in cash, but the dealer clearly was not. It was the perfect way to launder the money. A few members of his crew bring the drug money into the casino to this specific table with a dealer who is in on it, where they would lose big thus making the deposit of the ill-gotten gains. As owner of the casino, Perez profited from it and the money was cleaned without him ever touching it.

Unfortunately, casino security quickly picked up on Sloan and BT watching the gambling going on in a semi-private side room. Security then picked them up, escorting them into an employee's only corridor with the security interrogation room in the basement the final destination even though both men drew their badges. Sloan carried ATF credentials and BT carried FBI. The casino security didn't seem to care. That was when the two men figured out that these two, perhaps all of the security were in on the illegal drug money deposits.

"Listen, asshole," Sloan said once they were inside the inner employees only corridor and out of public view. "We have several more team members nearby and listening to this exchange. The only place you're escorting us is to the penthouse to see Perez. We know he's up there."

"Oh, fuck," Mother swore through their comms. "This is not keeping a low profile."

The two security guards exchanged unsure

glances.

"All I want for Christmas is to not get shot," the Birdman sang. "To not get shot, and that goes for you'all too. Careful, Undertaker. The missus will be pissed if we don't bring you home in one piece."

One of the two security guards transmitted their situation to the security control room to ask for directions.

Sitting in a car out in front of the casino alone, Michael Cooper knew that things were about to get a whole lot more complicated. "I hope you have a plan, Undertaker."

"I'm sure he does," Taco chimed in. "You going to play cop on the take, Undertaker? Or are you going to play it straight up agent in charge?"

"I'll call it into Ops," Mother transmitted.

***

At twenty-two hundred, Shepherd and Diana went to bed. They'd enjoyed a quiet night after dinner, relaxing on the couch seated beside each other, catching up on professional reading they both needed to. Once beneath the sheets. Hands roamed and their bodies pressed against each other, preparing for a night of passion that was long overdue. Their session was just getting interesting when it was interrupted by his phone chirping an alert.

"No," Diana moaned.

"I'm sorry," Shepherd said, rolling over to grab his phone from the bedside table. It was a priority alert from Ops. "Let me see if I can resolve it from here." He rolled back over and embraced her while he pressed dial and then clutched the phone to his ear.

"Sorry to have to alert you," Yvette said. "Something went down with Delta-Echo Team you need to be aware of."

"Tell me," Shepherd said.

"Mother reported that casino security picked up BT and the Undertaker. They didn't care that the two flashed their badges. The team suspects security and at least one dealer is involved in the money laundering."

"Where are Sloan and BT now?" Shepherd asked.

"They asked to be escorted to Perez's penthouse. Mother suspects the Undertaker is planning to run a cop on the take shakedown. Their communications with the team were cut off by some kind of sophisticated jamming equipment when Sloan and BT went upstairs."

"How long have they been out of communication with the team?" Shepherd asked.

This statement raised alarm with Diana. It didn't sound good. Sloan and BT could be in trouble.

"Five minutes," Yvette replied. "I've still got Mother on the line. Do you want to be patched in?"

"Affirmative." He sat up straight, flashing Diana an apologetic frown. A moment later Yvette advised they were connected. "Mother, does your gut tell you they're in trouble?"

Mother sighed. "I don't like that they're out of communication, but I trust that Sloan knows what he's doing. He told the guards that other members of the team were nearby and listening. I'd have to think Perez isn't dumb enough to kill two federal agents who have partners nearby and listening. He hasn't kept the drug trade away from himself by being stupid."

"Agreed. Do you have any other members of the team in the casino?"

"Affirm," Mother replied. "After the two were on the move to the penthouse, the Birdman and Taco entered the building. They're holding position on the ground floor near the elevator."

"Have them move into position on the floor below the penthouse and get one more asset inside to cover the elevators on the ground floor. And keep me informed on the situation. I want a call from the Undertaker and BT as soon as their clear."

"Yes, sir," Mother replied and then disconnected. He communicated the directions to the team and then he moved in to cover the ground floor elevators. Bubbles would remain in his vehicle in the parking lot, close to the front doors of the casino.

Up in the penthouse, BT and Sloan stood facing Germaine Perez, identifying themselves, badges, and creds in hand. His security personnel hadn't frisked them, hadn't taken their weapons. They hadn't even asked if they were armed. Some security.

"What do I owe the honor of this visit from the FBI and the ATF, gentlemen?" Perez said coolly, with a distinct Mexican accent. He was a diminutive man, stood no taller than five foot. He had a slight frame, dark skin, and a weathered face making him look older than his forty-five years. His hair was cut short, and he dressed in expensive clothes. He impersonated an upstanding citizen very well.

"Mister Perez," Sloan began, "Can we speak to you alone, please." He glanced over his shoulder at the two security guards who stood behind them.

"These two men are my most trusted. You can speak freely in front of them."

"Very well. There is a man downstairs playing at one of your tables who is the object of our investigation. He is a known arms dealer and extortionist," Sloan said. "We have reason to believe that he is in the process of a very big illegal arms deal and we've had him under surveillance. We're not sure if your security had him under surveillance when they homed in on us, but if they did, we need to know why."

"Is that a fact? An arms dealer?" Perez repeated dramatically.

"Yes. Now, why was your security staff watching that table, or more specifically us?"

"Not the two of you, gentlemen. I can assure you of that," Perez said.

Sloan and BT waited. Perez provided no more. They knew why security had picked them up and they knew he'd never admit to it. If any words did come out of him it would be a lie. But they still wanted to see what that lie would be. They remained silent, watching Perez with expectation.

Finally, Perez caved to the silence. "It was actually the dealer my security has under surveillance. The dealer is a woman, so I'm sure she is not the object of your investigation. It is an internal casino matter, so I cannot elaborate." He crossed the room and retrieved an iPad type of device. He brought up the casino security cameras focused on that table. "Can you please tell me which player is under your suspicion." He turned the screen so BT and Sloan could view it.

BT and Sloan exchanged glances. "I'm sorry, Mister Perez," BT said. "We cannot elaborate either."

"Then we are at a standoff," Perez said. "I thank you for your candor and your understanding of my internal situation. I will have my security staff escort you back to the casino floor. If you remain or leave is your prerogative. My security team will not interfere with you further. Have a nice day, gentlemen."

Echo

After Shepherd had ended the call with Mother, he kissed Diana. "There's no use us both losing sleep tonight." He got up and pulled a pair of sweat pants on. "I'm going to wait in my office for the call. It could come in fifteen minutes or fifty. I don't want to disturb your sleep. I know you have an early morning."

She reached her hand to him. "I love you, Sam."

He took her hand and crawled back onto the bed to give her another kiss. "I love you too. Thank you for putting up with the interruptions my job brings."

"If you didn't do this job, you wouldn't be you, the man I love. Go, make sure Sloan and BT are okay. You can wake me when you come back." She beamed him an inviting smile.

"You don't know how much I just want to crawl back under those sheets with you," he said.

"But you wouldn't be in the moment while

waiting for that call. After..." she assured him.

He left the room and walked down the hall to his home office to wait. He sat and opened his email on his computer. Might as well get some work done as he waited. It was only a half hour before the incoming phone call vibrated his cell phone against the desk. It was Sloan. "Shepherd," he answered.

"It's Sloan, Michael, and BT, Shep," Sloan said. They were in the car and had the phone on speaker. "The rest of the team is on comms." The Birdman, Mother, and Taco were still in the casino. They had moved to the floor where they could watch the participants at the table from a distance. It was no longer necessary to see the play. They already knew the players at the table were losing, thus making large deposits of drug money. They would follow the other players when they left.

"What happened?" Shepherd asked.

"Germaine Perez is smooth. He has quite the operation going," BT said. "His money runners sit at a specific table away from the main gaming area and lose heavily, even when their hands won over the dealer. She's in on it. This is how he's washing the money."

"He thinks he said all the right things to placate two federal agents, but he tipped his hand," Sloan said. "He just doesn't know it."

"Why did you engage?" Shepherd asked. "That wasn't your mission."

"No, but we'd already been made by his security, who are in on the drug money deposits. Had we not spoken up they would have searched us and found our weapons and creds. If we were there on a legit mission identifying ourselves and demanding to be brought to the owner was the only logical course," Sloan said.

Shepherd closed his eyes and rubbed between them. "Yes, you're right. How'd his security make you?"

"Watching that deposit game and who took an interest in it was all security was focused on. We could have robbed the cashiers, and no one would have said shit to us," BT said.

"How'd you play it with Perez?" Shepherd asked.

"Being the diligent agents we are," BT began, "we felt we needed to inform him that he had a known felon in his establishment."

"We had to make a split-second decision to be either legit agents or be agents on the take there to shake him down. If he doesn't think he's under any suspicion, we keep the upper hand by not going down that road. Better for him to think we're investigating something entirely different."

"His guard will be up now," Shepherd said.

"Yes, and he'll also be suspecting one of his crew is engaging in a side gig of his own. That's not going to go over well either," BT said. "Especially because he knows the man's history, knows he's a felon and was running guns before he went to prison and then hired by Perez."

"He may have his guard up, but I don't think he has a clue he's the focus of anything. My ATF creds take all suspicion away from me investigating gambling or drug crimes," Sloan said.

"True," Shepherd agreed. "What's your next move?"

"Mother, the Birdman, and Taco are inside watching the game from a distance. They shouldn't get made. They're not looking to see what's going down at the table, like we were. Then we're going to follow the other members of the game, the other runners who are making their deposits to get IDs on them. We'll send the info collected to the Digital Team to run them to ground," BT said.

"There are seven players including Salazar. How are six of you going to follow seven people?"

"We're banking on the two couples leaving together. If they separate, we'll follow one and hope to reacquire the other at a later date. I have to believe these games to deposit the drug money occur multiple times a week," BT said.

"And Perez?" Shepherd asked.

"He'll be out of surveillance for a short time. Anything damning regarding the money will be behind the employees only doors. We think following the other runners is more important right now," Sloan said.

"I agree. Let's get IDs on all of them," Shepherd said.

"Sloan will stay on Salazar, though we're sure Perez will tell him he's under surveillance, so it will be for show," BT answered. "We also need to get info on the two security guards who escorted us up to Perez. He called them his most trusted and I'm sure they are and in on it too."

"Agreed. The dealer and any of the security staff who were watching that table need to be ran to ground. Get as much info to the Digital Team that you can. Nice work," he said.

"Thanks, Shep," BT and Sloan both acknowledged.

After the call BT and Sloan re-entered the casino. Through comms, Mother broadcast. "One of the security guards that escorted you down went over and whispered something in our boy's ear after you left. He didn't look very happy to hear whatever it was."

"If I were a betting man, I'd wager it was a message to go see the big boss after the game," BT said. "He doesn't know it yet, but he's gonna have some 'splanin to do." He chuckled.

"Yeah, his boss is not going to be very happy with him. He may be in for a world of hurt," the Birdman said.

"I don't mean to be a dick, but not my problem," BT said.

"Nah, you can't help being a dick," the Birdman chimed in. "It just comes naturally." He laughed.

The team exchanged a bit more lighthearted banter, but they all knew that they very well could be getting Salazar killed. They'd be watching though, and if they could swoop in and prevent it from happening, they would, and it could get Salazar to flip on Perez.

Foxtrot

After the game ended, the house winning big, each man followed their target. As expected, Salazar disappeared behind the employees only door with the two security guards. The other male and one of the females who'd entered behind Perez exited the casino through the front doors. Bubbles, in his car in the parking lot, watched them get into a Ford Fiesta. He recorded the plates and then followed. The second couple slipped out through a back door that led to the employee parking lot. They were trailed by BT. He took surveillance pics of the car they got into, including the plates as he pretended to talk on his phone while crossing the parking lot to a random car. The solo man and the woman who'd entered with Salazar, left through different exits. Sloan followed one, Mother followed the other. Same routine with getting surveillance pics of them and their vehicles.

Meanwhile, Taco had also exited the front door of the casino and went to a second vehicle they had parked there. BT transmitted the make, model, and plates of the car the couple from the back lot drove away in. They were heading towards the main exit of the casino. Taco picked them up there and would follow them to wherever they went.

Likewise, the Birdman had also exited the casino even before the game ended. He was ready to cover another exit and follow any of the players. Sloan notified him of the heading of the man he followed, and the Birdman picked him up at the door. He got the info on his vehicle and followed him from the parking lot.

To help coordinate, Yvette and Smith were on at HQ.

Once the men BT and Sloan followed left, they returned to the casino floor just in time to see Salazar get off the elevator with Perez and his entourage. Salazar looked like he felt sick. They made a split-second decision. They rushed up to the group. Sloan drew his badge and creds. "Tomas Salazar, ATF, please come with us."

Perez momentarily looked angry. He schooled his reaction quickly. "Gentlemen, we were just escorting Mister Salazar from the premises. After your visit to me, I made the decision to have my security intercept him so we could advise him that he is banned from this establishment. We were just escorting him out."

Neither BT nor Sloan bought that. "We'll take custody of him," Sloan said.

Salazar looked confused but also relieved. "Am I under arrest?"

"You're being detained," Sloan replied. "You will receive specifics when we get you to the office." He removed his handcuffs from their position on his holster. "Hands behind your back, please."

Salazar's gaze went back and forth between Perez and Sloan for a moment before he complied. It was as though he wasn't sure which option was worse. As Sloan and BT led him out of the casino, Mother pulled up in the last rental vehicle they had. Sloan directed Salazar to sit in the back and he secured his seat belt. BT went around to the other side and slid into the back beside him. Then Sloan sat in the front passenger seat. Mother drove away. They knew there was camera surveillance on the front of the hotel. The car and Mother were also now made.

As they left the casino in their rearview mirror, Salazar was loudly protesting, demanding to be charged or released.

Sloan turned in his seat to look the man in the eye. "Listen up, Skits, we just saved your life. Your boss was going to have you killed."

Salazar's eyes went wide. "No."

Mother's gaze bounced to him for a second and then returned to the road. "We're your lifeline."

"I ain't no snitch," Salazar said. "And you ain't gonna be no lifeline without me being one."

"Perez accused you of running a big illegal arms deal that has the attention of the ATF and FBI, didn't he? Any law enforcement attention to his operation is the last thing he wants," Sloan said.

"You're a liability to him," BT added.

"The laundering of his drug money by you and the others who were at that blackjack table is more important to Perez than any person's life," Sloan said.

Salazar wasn't good at hiding his shock that they knew what the game had been about.

"Yeah, we know about his operation," BT said, drawing Salazar's startled gaze to him. "Right now, you've got to ask yourself, do you want to go down with him or do you want to come out of this on top?"

"Keep talking. I'm listening," Salazar said.

Golf

"You know what doesn't make sense?" Roth asked through comms.

Garcia and Doc were at the nearby hotel sleeping. The Shores, the casino resort they were investigating, was booked full. The team couldn't get a room at the last minute. Madison and Cooper were in the casino, pretending to play the slots, and Jackson was in the lobby looking through local tour flyers, waiting to see if their target, the resort's owner, Jonathan Burlington, made an appearance. Roth held position in the car in the parking lot watching the main entrance of the casino resort.

"In regard to what?" Jackson asked.

"It's colder than fuck out here," Roth said. "Who opens a new resort on the banks of Lake Michigan in November? He's got prime lakefront beach property and an amazing outdoor swimming pool complex. The timing of this opening last month makes no sense. If he wanted an opening to fill the bank, he would have timed it for the summer. One snowstorm off the lake, which happens often up here, and the whole area is paralyzed. He needs summer revenue to get him through the winter months. You've got the Blue Chip in Michigan City, and the Four Winds a few miles away. It's not like this is the only casino in the area."

"We'll have to have the Digital Team pull records to see if construction was delayed. Maybe it was set to open in June and fell far behind," Madison said.

"December is the month when people freely spend money," Jackson chimed in.

"Yeah, but that usually comes to a screeching halt in January," Cooper said. "Everyone is paying off their Christmas debt. If the construction didn't fall way behind, I think the timing is something we should consider given we have little else for this case."

Roth felt Cooper's frustration. No, they didn't have much to go on regarding this investigation. The financing of the resort was sketchy, but they didn't have any particulars on what was suspicious that the FBI was investigating. The CIA would not tell them who the coded emails were exchanged with, just that it was a foreign national in Dubai. What country was this person from? Had he been thoroughly investigated? Or were they in the process of investigating this person? Talk about trying to do this with their hands tied behind their backs, a blindfold on, and ear plugs.

"Is this normal on these kinds of cases, not knowing jack shit?" Roth asked.

"No, normally we get a bit more," Cooper answered. "Whoever he was corresponding with in code is a big fish they're still investigating. That's what all this secrecy is telling me."

"Damn is it cold out here," Roth repeated.

"Turn the engine on and blast the heat," Jackson said.

"It is on and on full blast," Roth said. "Has been the last hour. Whatever this guy is up to, it isn't outside."

Cooper gazed across the casino at the cashier's cages. The cashiers all wore short sleeved shirts and they looked bored. Only a few guests had approached them in the last hour. He glanced around the interior of the casino again. It wasn't crowded to capacity. "No, it's not," he said thoughtfully. "And Crash is right about the summer months funding the winter. It's very comfortable in here, even with the outside doors opening and closing all night as people come and go. The amount this guy is spending to heat this place has to be ridiculous."

"So, he's conducting some other business behind closed doors that's paying the bills," Jackson concluded.

"Yeah," Cooper agreed. "That would also explain why it isn't packed in here. If the hotel is fully booked, where are the people and what are they doing instead of gambling. Crash, come inside. We're going to need you," Cooper said.

Roth shut the engine down and exited the car, pulling his hat down over his ears and turning his collar up to shield his neck from the frigid chill. He hurried across the nearly full parking lot and entered through the front doors. "Yeah, the parking lot is full of cars," Roth said, his gaze sweeping the casino. "I expected this place to be packed."

"I'm going to walk down to the events area and see if the ballrooms are in use. Maybe there's something going on in there that is the big draw," Madison said.

"Yeah, and I'm going to go check out the inside pool areas," Jackson said.

Cooper made eye contact with Roth. "Let's drop your coat at the coat check and then go ride the elevator and mosey around each floor to take a looksee."

They waited by the elevator bank watching the numbers on the four elevators display what floor they were on or moving to. They noticed that two of them were not running. One of the other elevators arrived and opened. They stepped into the empty car. "Two elevators out of service in a brand-new hotel?" Cooper commented as a question.

"And there are no other elevators on the blue prints," Roth said.

Cooper knew that too. They'd studied the building blueprints on file in preparation for this case. There was the casino floor, two restaurants, ballrooms, and hotel tower consisting of ten floors, forty rooms to a floor, four hundred guest rooms. Assuming two to a room, there could be up to eight hundred guests booked into the hotel. Where the hell were all the people?

Cooper and Roth got off on each floor, walked the halls, and then returned to the elevator to go to the next floor. They'd repeat this until all ten floors were checked out. They only ran into a few people in the hallways, and they were dressed to the nines.

"Nothing going on at all in the ballroom wing," Madison reported.

"Pool area has a few moms with their kids swimming," Jackson chimed in. "And I passed by both restaurants. There are a few diners, not packed."

On the seventh floor, Cooper and Roth caught a break. As they had just arrived back at the bank of elevators to go up to the eighth floor, one of the elevator doors opened. An elderly, Japanese couple got off. It had come up from below. The two men entered the car only to discover there were no floor choice buttons. Just a card reader where a room card or some kind of card would be tapped.

"This was one of the cars out of service," Roth said.

"Out of public service maybe," Cooper said.

Cooper made a show of searching his pockets, knowing there would be a camera in the car. "Do you have the keycard," he said to Roth, his eyes conveying to play along.

Roth did the same, making a show of looking for the keycard. Just then, the elevator door opened, and another man entered. He was Middle Eastern. He pulled a keycard from his pocket. It clearly was not a room key as the room key cards had the hotel's name on it. This one was black with a silver swish across it.

"And ours would be sitting on the table in our room," Cooper said to the man.

He nodded and then tapped his card. The doors closed and the elevator descended. Digital display numbers counted down the floors, six, five, four, three, two, ground, S-1, S-2. When the doors opened, they followed the man from the elevator, stepping out into an elegant foyer.

They followed him into the main room. The massive room before them was lit from crystal chandeliers spaced across the mural painted ceiling. In front of them lay rows and rows of gaming tables. A fancy bar ran the length of the room to the right. At the far end of the right side was a seating area with expensive-looking furniture. And the place was packed with people.

"Whoa," Roth remarked aloud.

"We hit paydirt," Cooper transmitted.

There was no answer.

"I didn't even hear you through comms," Roth said.

"There's a jammer," they said in unison.

Hotel

On the casino floor, Madison went back to the slots. An older Japanese woman sat beside her. She looked disgusted. "The one-armed bandits getting the better of you tonight?" she asked the woman, making conversation.

"Maybe they'll treat me better than the tables have tonight," she answered with a heavy Japanese accent. "I prefer slots, anyway. It is my husband who likes the high-stakes tables. I don't have the will for it."

"I agree," Madison said. "My husband loves blackjack, usually does quite well. This is fine for me." She spun the wheels with the button again.

"I left him down there and came up to make reasonable bets," she said.

Madison wasn't sure if it was her English skills that made her say up and down, rather than over here or over there, but she doubted it. Down there? That had to be it. There was a second casino, probably an illegal one downstairs someplace. "Please excuse me," she said to the woman. She got up and hurried away. "Coop, I think there's a second casino in the basement."

She waited. There was no answer from Cooper.

"Xena, where are you now?" Jackson's voice came through comms.

"I just lifted a server's apron and I'm going to slip into the kitchen to poke around for another elevator or see if the kitchen elevator takes me there," she reported. "Coop and Crash aren't answering."

"I'm on my way. Is there a second apron I can slip on?" Jackson asked. "We need to find the team."

"I'll bet they found it first and there are jammers interfering with our comms. They wouldn't want any of their players having cell service."

"Agreed," said Jackson.

She gave him directions to where she was. After he'd donned the server's apron, they strode into the kitchen like they belonged. Several other servers were loading their trays at the food prep station. They followed suit. Then they fell in behind the others who took an escalator down to the floor beneath them, the basement. There, the trays were set on a conveyor that descended one more floor. Voices, laughter, and other sounds that proved there was a crowd one floor below them echoed up.

"We have to get down there," Jackson whispered to her.

"There has to be a staff staircase," Madison said. "They wouldn't be using the same elevator the guests use and I doubt they would have spent the money to build an elevator just for the employees."

They searched the level they were on and found nothing.

"It has to be somewhere back here in the employee area," Madison said.

"I'm thinking near security," Jackson said. "It will have controlled access."

They took the up escalator back to the kitchen. From there they took the hallway into the bowels of the interior of the staff space. Tucked in one of the corners, they found a staircase that led down. They took the stairs down two flights, coming into a small kitchen prep area. It was bustling with activity. Exiting it, they found themselves in the hallway the restrooms were in. They ditched the aprons behind a large potted plant and then stepped out onto the casino floor.

***

On the illegal casino floor, Cooper became aware that they were being watched by who he assumed were security. They were dressed in black suits over crisp white dress shirts and sported ear pieces. He and Roth casually stepped over to the bar.

"May I see your black cards, please?" the bartender asked as he came in front of them.

"Left mine up in the room," Cooper said. He glanced around. "Where's my wife?" He shot the handsome bartender a smile. "You know women, always disappearing. She has hers."

"The terms were disclosed to you. All must have their own card on them at all times," the bartender said.

"Oh, I didn't know you'd be sticklers. Okay, will have to go get it."

He and Roth stepped away from the bar and wound their way through the tight knot of players on the floor, heading back to the elevator. He had seen a call button outside of the car. He hoped they could easily leave.

Just as they reached the foyer the elevator was in, two of the men they assumed to be security stepped in front of them. "Excuse me sir, may I see your black cards?"

"Just going back to the room to get them. My

wife had hers. I thought that was good enough," Cooper said.

"And where is she now?" The guy wasn't buying it.

"In the ladies room."

The man's eyes went across the floor to the hallway that led to the restrooms.

Cooper and Roth saw Madison and Jackson step into the casino from the hallway. "There she is," Cooper said. He took his phone from his pocket and brought up a picture of the two of them together. He showed the security guard. "Me and the missus." He smiled.

The man viewed the picture and then his gaze went back to Madison. "Sorry to have bothered you, sir. Please do go to your room at your convenience and retrieve your black cards."

"Sure will, sorry to have accidentally broken the rules," Cooper said. Then he and Roth made a beeline to Madison and Jackson. Upon arriving at their location, he wrapped an arm around her. "Great timing, honey. Glad you're here but it's time to go."

The four of them walked back to the elevators and rode it until they opened up on a guest floor having been called by another guest. They switched to another elevator to ride it to the ground floor. There, they all retrieved their coats from the coat check station.

Once out in the frigid night air, Cooper pulled his phone from his pocket and called into Ops. He made his report that Shepherd would forward to the proper agency so the illegal casino would be raided and shut down by the proper authorities. Not bad. Three days on the ground and they'd wrapped it up. More than likely, they would head home the following morning.

Indigo

Alpha Team met with the FBI, the Attorney General, and the Michigan Gaming Control Board at zero nine hundred the following morning and detailed out their findings at The Shores Casino. Shepherd was dismayed when he'd spoken with Leonard Whiting, the Deputy Director of the FBI, his contact, the previous evening. Whiting took the information from him and when he reached back out, he notified Shepherd that the Michigan Attorney General would not act on the FBI's report without speaking to the team that discovered the illegal gambling operation. And he would not see the members of Alpha Team to receive their report until the next morning. Shepherd found this delay unacceptable.

On the schematics for the casino, Cooper and Madison showed the authorities where the second sub-basement was accessed from the ground floor. They also described the elevator system and the black cards with the silver swish on it for guest access. Cooper had managed to capture a few photos on his phone of the basement gambling area in the few moments he had his phone out, showing that security person the picture of Madison and himself.

The Attorney General sanctioned a raid on the casino sub-basement level as only one gaming floor of a specified square footage, a discrete number of tables, and an exact number of slot machines was licensed. In Cooper's pictures, it was clear that the number of tables in the photo exceeded the number of tables the casino was licensed to operate. The raid would not take place until that evening when the casino would be the most crowded. The team was asked to remain in town to consult during the raid.

"I'm not sure what you could possibly need to consult with us about," Madison said. "We've shown you proof of the operation in the pictures. We've detailed out the operation and guest admittance as well as pinpointed how the employees access the private area. This is all but tied up in a big red Christmas bow for you."

"Agent Miller, I appreciate that," the Attorney General began. "Please understand my need to be sure all the Is are dotted and all Ts are crossed. If we run into anything unexpected, having the team who discovered the operation on site could be helpful. When we go in, I want to hit the jackpot and get them with no doubt as to the illegal nature of the venture."

"I'll need to consult with my boss to be sure he will grant us permission to remain on site and be a party to the raid," Cooper said.

***

"Jeez, shut the fuck up and stop whining already," Sherman snapped at Salazar, his Cajun accent making the words sound harsh. He sat beside him in the backseat of the car. "Either you're going through with it or you're not. Make a decision and stick with it. If you don't go through with it, we'll drop you back off at the casino in front of Perez's cameras and make a good show of thanking you for all the information and we'll look all chummy."

"You can't do that. He'll have me killed," Salazar argued.

"You agreed to give a full statement to the DEA in exchange for immunity from prosecution. A full statement means names, dates, addresses, phone numbers, the how's, where's, and why's. All of it," Sloan said. That's why we're here. To deliver you to the DEA who will take that statement."

"I was high when I agreed. Certainly, that voids my agreement," Salazar said.

"The U.S. Marshals Service will keep you protected. You will be given a new identity and be relocated far from here, giving you your one chance to start your life over. You can leave all this behind and be a normal guy. Come on Skits, make a smart, honest move. You'll never get this chance again," Mother said.

"I know you're right. I just can't get past that I'm going to be a snitch."

"Don't you think it's better to be a live snitch rather than a dead stand-up guy?" Sloan asked.

"Okay, okay, I'll make a full statement."

And with that agreement, Sloan, Mother, and Sherman got him out of the car and walked him into the Shelby County Justice Center through the secure attached garage structure on Poplar Avenue in Memphis, Tennessee. They'd kept him at the hotel with them the night before, talking him into making the statement. Now they would turn him over and their involvement in this case was closed. They would meet the Lear at the airfield at eleven hundred hours.

***

Shepherd approved Alpha Team's involvement in the raid. The six of them would all don FBI vests and accompany the other agents. The raid was set for twenty-one hundred hours. The Shepherd Security Team and Agent Farmer strategized the handling of the raid. It had to be from two directions, the employee staircase, and the guest elevators. That meant, they'd have to intercept a guest who had a black card. They'd have to obtain it and fill an elevator with agents.

"Security needs to be neutralized for that to happen either by knocking out the cameras or taking over the security office," Garcia said. "Security sees agents and they notify their guys down in the casino. There could be six other ways out of there that we don't know about, and we could storm in to bust an empty room."

"That'll happen anyway the second they see agents and police enter the casino," Farmer said.

"Then they don't see us until it's too late for them to do anything," Cooper said.

From twenty thirty hours to twenty forty hours the six members of the Shepherd Security Team, Agent Farmer and three other FBI agents entered the casino through the front doors in five groups of two. Madison, Jackson, and Garcia met up near the entrance to the kitchen Madison and Jackson had used the previous night to gain access to the sub-basement casino. They were dressed like the waitstaff to blend in. Garcia was dressed like the floor security personnel in a black suit over a white dress shirt.

According to the schematics, the main security monitoring room was accessible from the employee area they'd been in the night before. They now knew which door led into that room. They assumed the tech that jammed the communications frequencies in the secret casino would be controlled in the monitoring room as well.

The seven others took the two public elevators to place themselves on different guest room floors. Their job was to secure a black card from a hotel guest either going to or returning from the illegal casino and be ready to descend to the illegal gaming floor to commence the raid. A dozen other agents waited in vehicles at the edge of the parking lot, ready to stream in when the security cams were offline.

In front of the door to the security monitoring room, Madison and Jackson acted out a lover's quarrel with loud voices, curses, and some pushing and shoving. A camera was in the hallway giving the security personnel a good view of what took place outside their door. As expected, one of the security personnel entered the hallway from the casino floor to move the two along and de-escalate the situation.

Before he was in camera range, Garcia intercepted him, badge and gun drawn. "Nope, freeze right here. You're going to get us into the control room. We're serving a warrant but don't want everyone to know it yet. You got me?"

The man nodded and raised his arms. "I'm not armed."

"You're not under arrest unless you resist or try to tip off security."

The man nodded.

"How many are inside the monitoring control room?" Garcia asked.

"There's always two."

"You have a key or access?"

"Yes, it's a code entry lock. I have the code."

"Very good. You're going to get us in and then step to the wall inside. Is the owner on site tonight?" Garcia asked.

"Not that I'm aware of but he doesn't clear his schedule with me."

"Watch that attitude," Garcia warned. "You're starting to sound uncooperative."

"No not at all," he swore.

"There is a jammer preventing electronic communication on the basement gambling floor. Where is that controlled from?"

"It's in the pit boss' office down there," he answered.

"Okay, I'm going to put my weapon away and you and I are going to confront the disturbance and send them on their way and then you're going to open the monitoring room door and we go in."

It played out just that way. Garcia kept his back to the camera so the guards inside wouldn't see his face. Madison and Jackson waited just out of the camera's range. As soon as the door was open, they rushed forward, entering just behind Garcia. They announced themselves as federal agents serving a warrant and quickly pulled the two men from their chairs, securing all three of the casino employees against the wall. Garcia took one of the chairs and got to work securing the camera feeds.

"We're in control of the monitoring room," Madison broadcast after they were sure it was secure. "And we have a black card if you haven't acquired one yet. But the bad news is the jammer controls are downstairs. We can't turn it off from here."

"Thank you, Xena, but we have secured one," Cooper replied. He was on the fourth floor and a guest who'd lost big in the illegal establishment was happy to hand it over. One of the FBI agents would remain with him to ensure he alerted no one. The rest of the team, Farmer, and his other agents all waited with Cooper and the men from Shepherd Security.

Farmer transmitted the go order to the agents in the parking lot. They drove up beside the employee entrance in the back of the kitchen area where Madison let them in and escorted them to the stairs to access the illegal gaming area. The timing of the raid was coordinated between them and the men on the fourth floor. Before they called the private elevator, they removed their jackets and affixed the patch with the letters FBI to the vests they wore beneath. They were ready.

"We're stepping into the elevator now," Farmer transmitted. "Move into position and go when you hear us."

Inside the elevator as it descended, the six men pulled their badges and weapons to be ready. When the doors opened on sub-basement level two, Cooper and Farmer led the others out. It only took a second for them to be seen coming into the foyer and then the gambling floor. A hush came over those assembled as they were seen. It washed over the crowd, beginning as a ripple and cresting like a tsunami. The hush then morphed into pandemonium.

The dozen other agents entered through the rear near the restrooms. Though a few of the employees darted towards the back stairs, where Madison and one of the agents waited to intercept them, no one else tried to flee. They had the room locked down in a matter of minutes.

The warrant was served, the establishment shut down. The owner was located at his Memphis estate in a gated neighborhood. The AG proclaimed the raid a success and filed official charges. It was just after zero one hundred when the Shepherd Security Team was clear from the scene. A storm was blowing across Lake Michigan and would have the area shut down by morning. With this case successfully closed, the team decided to make the three-hour drive home rather than potentially being stranded in New Buffalo the next day.

Juliette

December 15th Friday night, 9 days before Christmas Eve

After Angel and Jackson had tucked the kids in bed for the night, they snuggled on the couch watching a movie. The alert coming from his phone made them both groan. They both knew the sound well. He reached for his phone, which was on the table beside him. He checked the display to confirm what they both knew to be true. Yes, his team had been scrambled.

"Sorry, babe," Jackson said. He pressed a kiss to her lips before he stood.

Angel came to her feet as well. "Better tonight than closer to Christmas. Whatever it is, you should be able to resolve it and be home before Christmas Eve."

Jackson kissed her again. "I'd assume so."

Another incoming text chimed on his phone. It was Garcia offering to give both him and Doc a ride to the office. Jackson replied yes, with a thank you. Doc's reply chimed in next. He would catch a ride with Cooper and Madison when they came to drop Hahna off.

"So, it must be big if Madison got scrambled too," Jackson said. "She's supposed to be at HQ for the rest of the month."

An uneasy feeling settled in the pit of Angel's stomach. "Yes, it must be. Be safe. I love you," she whispered in his ear as she gave him one final embrace.

"I love you and the kids. You're my life. Always remember that my Angel. I'll let you know what's up when I can." And then with one more kiss to her lips, he donned his jacket and grabbed his go-bag.

The cool night air invigorated Jackson as he crossed the street in a brisk pace to Garcia and Sienna's house. Even though he loved Angel and the kids with all his heart, he also loved the job. The adrenaline that spiked when an alert scrambled the team, got his blood pumping and his mind focused. Garcia had just backed out of his garage. He tossed his backpack in the backseat and then slid into the passenger seat beside Garcia.

"You got any idea what's up?"

"No. When I was at the office earlier today, all was quiet," Garcia said. "All I can say is I'm glad it was tonight and not closer to Christmas."

Jackson had to laugh at his statement. He was sure the other team members with children were all thinking the same thing. "I'm sure we'll be back by Christmas."

"Yeah, we better be," he agreed.

They drove in silence the remainder of the way to HQ. But when they saw the line of vehicles entering the parking garage beside the Shepherd Security building, curses flew from each of their mouths. Ahead of them, Jackson counted six familiar vehicles. And four more quickly filled in behind them.

"Oh, fuck," Jackson cursed. "That's Mother's pickup up there and I'm pretty sure Wilson's truck already passed through the gates."

"Three full teams. Can't be good," Garcia agreed.

Once they'd passed through the gate, and both garage doors, they pulled into the private Shepherd Security garage, which was full of vehicles and men. Jackson had been correct. Jimmy Wilson's pickup was parked, and he stood near the elevator talking with Mother, Sebastian Roth, and BT. The others were grabbing their gear from their vehicles.

"Make that four full teams," Jackson said. "Looks like Echo was called in too."

"Oh, fuck me," Garcia moaned. "Whatever it is, is really bad."

Garcia parked and the two men quickly grabbed their bags. They joined the others who were gathering near the elevator and stairwell door. There was a hum, an electricity, crackling through the men. Everyone knew it was something big. Even though the men knew that something dire had taken place for four teams to be scrambled, this is what they were trained for. This is why they existed, to respond in dire situations. And they all knew this team was the best.

The elevator arrived and many piled in. Garcia and Jackson and several others took the stairs up to the fifth floor where the pre-Op briefing would take place in the large hallway conference room. They arrived just after the elevator. They followed the stream of men down the hall. Filing into the room, they saw that Lambchop was there, seated at the conference table with Shepherd. On the monitor was a map of the Nuba Mountains in Africa, specifically the southern region of Sudan.

This just went from bad to worse. Sudan had been thrust into a violent civil war nine months earlier with fighting between the Sudan Armed Forces (SAF) and the paramilitary Rapid Support Forces (RSF). Civilians who hadn't fled were being killed daily, collateral damage of the fighting. In the first weeks of fighting, the US State Department with US Department of Defense assistance, helped to evacuate all Americans who wanted to leave.

"Get settled, gentlemen. We have a lot to cover," Shepherd said. "You're wheels up in an hour."

The last few trickled in, including Doc, Cooper, and Madison. Everyone's eyes were glued to the monitor.

"You all know the ongoing situation in Sudan. While all official government personnel and most of the U.S. citizens were evacuated during the first few weeks of the conflict last April, it is estimated over a thousand U.S. citizens remain, mostly those who hold dual citizenship," Shepherd began. He clicked the keys on his monitor and the map zoomed in. "This is what is left of one of the largest villages in the Kordofan region in the Nuba Mountains that had gone untouched until now. It was attacked less than a day ago. What's noteworthy about this village is that it's a Christian village. There was a five person U.S. missionary team in the area, against State Department directives. They have gone missing with the remainder of the occupants of this village that weren't killed."

The picture displayed was a still that had

been made from the camera on a drone as it had made a low pass over the village. It showed thatched roof huts clustered together in a circle. The majority of the roofs were burned, many still smoldered. At least half of the huts were completely destroyed. Dead bodies of humans and animals lay in the destruction.

"Do we have positive IDs on the dead to know they are not among them?" Cooper asked.

"That's the odd thing, there were very few casualties, and they were all local villagers," Shepherd answered.

"Do we have any idea where the villagers are?" Madison asked.

"One of two theories prevail. Either they retreated into the mountains and are hiding, or they were taken by their attackers, presumed to be one side of the conflict or the other. Neither side claims the region as theirs," Shepherd answered. "U.S. Intelligence experts believe it was SAF forces. If they took those villagers, they are in military prep camps being trained to fight."

"And those who won't fight will be executed," Lambchop added.

"Either way, those people are someplace up in the mountains. We'll use satellites and drones to search for them, but those mountains have a lot of caves where neither tech will find them. With that being said, someone has to be out on patrol of the area or sentries will be positioned near the mouth of the cave. Thermal imaging satellites will catch them and then we can check out the surrounding area for the rest, be it refugees or the aggressive force that took them," Shepherd said.

"Have we been cleared to engage?" Cooper asked.

"Affirmative. We're sanctioned to use lethal force if needed to rescue the refugees and relocate them to a camp where they can receive humanitarian aid," Shepherd said. "And the missionaries can choose if they will remain or be evacuated out of Sudan."

"You said we're wheels up in an hour?" Garcia asked.

"You'll catch a hop on an aircraft that's been brought in to transport you over to the arena out of the O'Hare military hangar. You'll change planes in Tampa with your flight plan finally delivering you to Djibouti, which will be the base you'll operate from, running two team missions into the target area around the clock until those villagers are located. Jackson, Saxton will remain at HQ to help man Ops. You'll be on loan as the fourth member of Echo. Alpha and Echo will be paired as will Delta and Charlie."

Jackson acknowledged him with a nod. He

was hyper focused and ready to get to work.

"We'll plan the rotation and mission details on our flight over," Cooper said.

"Grant is pulling your ammo. Handguns and assault rifles. And you're to wear dog tags. This is an official mission request from the DoD. That's it. Go find these people and deliver them to the refugee camp," Shepherd said.

Kilo

The team quickly loaded their gear and piled into four of the agency vehicles. They rolled out of the garage and drove the short distance to the airport. Each of the men with a significant other sent their loved one a text message that indicated their destination as a generic 'overseas', probable duration 'could extend to a few weeks', and they reiterated their love for their family. They promised to text or call when they could. That was all they could divulge of the operation.

Jackson stared for a few moments at a picture on his phone of Angel and the kids after he'd sent his text message to her. He knew she handled everything at home when he was on a mission. He never worried about her or the kids, he just missed them while he was gone, not that he wanted to give up field work entirely. The approximately fifty percent home, fifty percent away was working well, but that didn't make him miss them less when he wasn't home.

When they arrived at the military hangar at O'Hare International Airport their transport had just landed. As the C-23 Sherpa rolled towards them, Mother smiled. "I see regular seats through the windows. We won't be belting into the fuselage." They all knew that meant there was a possibility of grabbing a nap in comfort on the flight to Tampa, where at McDill Air Force Base, they'd most likely transfer to a C-17 or C-5 for the flight to Ramstein Air Force Base. Those seats would most likely be sidewall seats and not very comfortable.

They transferred their gear onto the plane and then climbed in, each claiming a seat. The seats were configured two, aisle, one. They only shared the plane with the pilots and crates of cargo strapped in the back. It was a very comfortable flight to Tampa.

Madison sat beside Cooper and laid her head onto his shoulder. His head was cushioned against the fuselage. They both slept soundly. Roth sat in the single seat across the aisle from them. He remembered when he'd met this team, during a special training exercise when he had just finished his SEAL training several years before. He recalled being stunned then to learn that they were married and operating together. His thoughts drifted to the woman he'd met on the CIA case he'd worked right after Thanksgiving. She could have fit in with the team to be his Madison. She was tough enough and former military. He'd wished he could have reached her.

Further back in the aircraft, Garcia was awake and had his tablet open. Mother sat with his head leaning against the fuselage beside him. Every other member of their team was asleep. The interior lights were dimmed. Only the glow cast from Garcia's tablet partially lit the cabin. As the plane began its descent into McDill, Mother woke. He leaned in, and his eyes took in what Garcia was working on. He was laying out search sectors of the most likely mountainous areas with cavernous faults in the ground penetrating radar sweep of one of the drones. These were areas where their targets could be hiding.

"I figure we send the drone back in as low as possible to pass over the areas with possible caves and have the camera on live mode with thermal cameras so we can look for heat signatures. If anyone is spotted, we have two teams in the area on a chopper to get dropped into the area for a looksee."

"If they were taken by those who attacked the village, we'll need more than eight of us to deal with them, especially announcing our presence with a chopper coming in," Mother said.

"Not necessarily," Garcia argued. "If we think the SAF have them squirreled away in a cave, we jam their communications as we approach and have our snipers take out the lookouts and patrols if there are any. Then we pop a few flashbangs into the cave followed by an anticholinergic laden device to temporarily incapacitate everyone inside. We go in with masks."

"Each team will have two medics in case anyone inside has a bad reaction to the agent. It will work if we can get approval to use it on the civilians," Mother agreed.

"That's if the SAF has them. My gut is telling me they're hiding up there," Garcia said.

"Yeah, mine too," Mother said. "Given that there are five American missionaries with them, if we don't see armed soldiers up there, but rather just villagers, I say we broadcast a message in English that we're the American Military there to rescue them and see what response we get. Get in there, rescue them, and get the hell out of Dodge."

Garcia smiled. "And home in time for Christmas."

"Yeah. Annaka and I fly in to see my family on Christmas Day."

"How's things between her and her mom?" Garcia asked. He knew that relationship was what was delaying the two of them getting married.

"I thought we were making headway, but her mother can't seem to dislodge her head from being up her ass."

Garcia chuckled.

"I swear that woman has no spine," Mother added. "And her husband is a controlling piece of shit."

"That's some way to talk about your future in-laws," Garcia said with a laugh. "Have you considered just saying fuck it and get married without her mom there?"

"If her mom doesn't come around by the spring, I think we will," Mother said. "I just don't want Annaka to have any regrets."

The team transferred to a C-17 at McDill in Tampa for the long flight to Ramstein. They settled into the uncomfortable sidewall seats, facing a mound of cargo lashed to the floor. Upon reaching cruising altitude, each member of the team enveloped themselves in their thermal blankets to stay warm in the unheated cargo bay of the plane. Garcia went over what he'd been working on with Cooper and Lambchop, who liked the plan.

The flight was long, but uneventful. They were on the ground for just enough time to refuel in Ramstein before the last leg of their journey brought them to Djibouti.

Lima

Kaylee Sloan hated to miss work. She truly loved her job teaching music at the elementary school that she was lucky to have gotten a job at. As usual, a flu bug was making its way through the school, and it had hit her the night before after dinner. She'd made herself a wonderful cobb salad only to throw all of it up an hour later. Her stomach remained unsettled all night. And here she was the next morning, waking and feeling just fine, but the tea and bagel she ate for breakfast came right back up.

On top of that, she felt exhausted and achy. Even her breasts ached. Yes, her period was a few weeks late, but she doubted she was pregnant. It had been erratic since her pregnancy and the miscarriage at nine weeks she'd suffered earlier in the year. She still mourned the loss of that baby.

Through the remainder of the day, the nausea came and went. But the level of exhaustion never changed, despite sleeping the majority of the day. It was later that night, after she made herself a dinner of buttered noodles, which she promptly threw up, that she decided to take a home pregnancy test, just to rule it out.

The line in the window turned pink immediately. Pregnant. "Oh, my God," she said aloud. A giddy feeling overtook her, and she began to cry happy, excited tears. But then the dread settled over her. She dropped to her knees at her bed and clasped her hands, bowing her head. "Dear God, please let me carry this one to term. Please let this baby be born." She said the Lord's Prayer and then rose from the floor, trying to bring some peace to her thoughts. Her phone rang, and she rushed to it, hoping it was Gary. Viewing the display, she saw it was Elizabeth. A small grin formed on her lips. "Thank you, God," she said out loud before answering the phone. Elizabeth was just who she needed to talk to. "Hello."

"Hi, how are you feeling?" Elizabeth asked. "Sienna told me you were sick and called in today."

Warmth spread through Kaylee's heart. She and Gary had agreed that when she got pregnant again, they'd tell no one. But she believed that God had brought this phone call to her at this moment, and she knew Gary would not mind her telling Elizabeth. Elizabeth could bring her that peace she needed. "I thought I had a touch of that flu that's been going around school. Well, I may, but I just took a test and I'm pregnant, Elizabeth. I haven't even told Gary yet."

"Kaylee, that's fantastic. Congratulations," Elizabeth exclaimed.

"I'm worried, Elizabeth. What if I lose this one too?"

"Don't think that way. You have to have faith. God will give you a baby in His time when the time is right for you. You have to have faith that now is that time." She heard her friend crying through the phone. "Just pray and enjoy knowing there is life inside you. This is a time to celebrate!"

"I know," Kaylee said. "I don't want to be worried and possibly doom this pregnancy too. I know a happy mom makes a happy baby and that stress can cause problems during pregnancy."

Elizabeth knew this thinking was toxic. If she were to lose the baby, she'd be sure it was her worry and anxiety that caused it. Elizabeth said a prayer into her phone hoping it would help to calm her friend. "Positive thoughts only," she said after concluding the prayer. "The fact that you are throwing up is good, the sign of a healthy pregnancy."

"Yes, I know. And the line turned bright pink right away so that means there's a lot of HCG in my system, another sign of a healthy pregnancy."

"That's right," Elizabeth insisted. "Do some mindful meditation whenever you're feeling anxious and visualize yourself at nine months pregnant and delivering a healthy baby. That should help bring you peace."

"That's a good idea," Kaylee agreed. "I'll actually do that now."

"And call Doctor Norman's office tomorrow and get yourself an appointment. Let me know if you want me to go with you and I'll have Dahlia cover for me babysitting. Take it easy and drink a lot of water."

Kaylee laughed, a smile spreading over her face and bringing a sparkle to her eyes. "Yes, Mom, I'll take care of myself."

Elizabeth laughed as well. "Call me if you need anything. And truly, congratulations."

"Thank you. Can you do me a favor though? Don't tell anyone else yet, okay?"

"I promise you I won't until you tell me otherwise."

Kaylee sat cross-legged on the bed and closed her eyes to meditate on a healthy baby, her and Gary welcoming him or her and holding the blanket-wrapped bundle in her arms. Elizabeth was right, positive thoughts only. She breathed deeply and relaxed every muscle in her body, allowing joy to wash through her. She couldn't wait to tell Gary.

Mike

Wednesday, December 20th

"Shepherd promised me the team would be home by Christmas," Angel said. She patted Ollie's head, who sat obediently on her rug. She was in Evie's veterinary clinic which took up one of the prime rental units on the first floor of the Shepherd Security Building. It was the only space with an outside entrance. "You're such a good girl," she said to the mostly black Belgian Malinois.

"I know they haven't even been gone a week yet," Evie said, breathing out a heavy sigh as she searched for the words to complete the sentence. "Maybe I'm not cut out to be with someone who does this for a living. I've had a really bad feeling since Brody left. Are they on their way back yet?"

"No, not that I'm aware of," Angel said. "But it's only about a twenty-hour flight, door to door with a stop in Germany to refuel and changing planes in Tampa. And you haven't been with BT for that long. It may take a little more time to get used to this." She didn't want Evie to psych herself out of being with BT because she didn't think she could handle it.

"I know, and thank you," Evie said. "I just can't shake this feeling of dread that came over me when he walked out the door. That hasn't happened since I've been here, and it hasn't let up."

"Have you talked with Joe Lassiter since they left?" Angel asked.

"No, I don't think it's related to my past trauma."

"It doesn't have to be," Angel said. "Evie, he's there for any issues, not just what happened to you."

"I just want to feel normal, Angel. Can you understand that? I don't want to feel like this mentally fragile freak."

Angel laughed. "I completely get that. And you're not a freak. As far as if you're mentally fragile or not, stop being so hard on yourself. What you went through was huge. It may take longer to work through it. It took me six months to almost feel like my old self after what happened to me. And there's nothing wrong with admitting that you may still be affected."

"Thank you. I know you're right, but really this feeling I've had ever since Brody left on this mission has nothing to do with what happened to me."

"I know you've spent time with Dahlia and Brielle since you moved here. Have you talked with them about how you feel?"

"I haven't seen them since the guys left on this mission. I was supposed to have dinner with them Sunday evening, but I cancelled because I had such a bad headache, probably from worrying."

"The only way we all get through these rough spots is by spending time together. All the wives and girlfriends are there for each other. I'm here for you. Please know you can call any of us at any time if you're feeling so worried that you're giving yourself a headache."

Evie gave her a hug and thanked her. She promised to reach out to her, Dahlia, Brielle, or any of the others if she felt that worried again. She also agreed to call Joe Lassiter if the overwhelming feeling of dread remained with her.

After Angel left the veterinary clinic, she took the elevator back to the fifth floor to return to her office. While in the elevator she sent Jackson a text message confirming she'd talked with Evie. Jackson had made the request of her as a favor to BT who was worried about Evie. Just as she returned to her desk, her phone rang an incoming call from Jackson. "Hello," she excitedly answered.

"Hi babe," Jackson said. "I love you and miss you and the kids."

"We love you and miss you too."

"We're just about to head back out. BT says thank you for checking in on her. He said she sounded very off in her text messages as well as when he talked to her yesterday. Is she okay?"

"Yes, tell BT she's fine. This is new to her, him getting an emergency scramble and deploying overseas. Tell him not to worry about her. We've got her. I'm going to reach out to Brielle and Dahlia and make sure one of us checks on her daily until you guys are back."

"Thanks. I'll let him know. How are the kids?"

"Missing their daddy as much as I am," Angel said. "But we're all fine. I bought the rest of the Christmas presents. Sammy is going to love that train you picked out. It is so cool."

"Yeah, I thought he would. I honestly can't wait to play with it with him," Jackson said with a chuckle.

He waved to Cooper, acknowledging that the team was getting ready to depart the hangar. The helicopters were ready to bring them back out to the search grid they'd tackle today. They were making progress, had eliminated a vast swath of mountainous terrain as possible locations the villagers were at.

Angel laughed too. "I thought it was more for you than him."

"Hey, listen babe, I have to go. The choppers are ready for us. I'll text you later when we return to base."

"Okay, I'm glad you got in a call. We love you, Jackson. Be safe."

"Always. I love you guys more than you'll ever know. I'll talk to you soon."

Angel stared at her phone after Jackson had disconnected. She would never share that Evie was worried or that she had a bad feeling. BT certainly didn't need to have anything to worry about at home. Angel respected that the team's focus had to be on the job they were doing. She always portrayed things at home as fine to Jackson when he was away, even if they weren't. She knew she could handle anything at home while he was away. He didn't need to be burdened. She would always tell him when he got home, including what she'd done to handle the situation or concern.

November

Jackson hurried to catch up with the team, who were exiting the hangar through the door that led to the flight line. Two Black Hawk helicopters waited to bring Alpha and Echo Teams to the search grids they'd fly over and investigate this evening.

The sun had set an hour earlier, and the night sky was clear, displaying thousands of stars against the inky heavens. The waning gibbous moon glowed bright enough to shine some celestial light on their search area. The temperature had cooled to a comfortable seventy-five degrees. It was a beautiful night.

As Alpha Team climbed aboard one chopper, Jackson, temporarily assigned to Echo Team, climbed aboard the other with BT, Bubbles, and Crash. He took up position near one of the doors opposite Crash at the other to provide cover. After liftoff, the two choppers headed west towards Sudanese airspace. The pilots were the same two men who'd flown their missions every night since they'd arrived. Alpha Team's pilots were the same who'd flown them as well.

Once over the mountain range the two choppers separated, each heading to the evening's search grids. "Coming up on station," the pilot's voice came through Echo Team's headphones. The aircraft's speed dramatically decreased.

In the back of the chopper, BT had his tablet open. He and Michael viewed the heat signature data that had been picked up by the drone pass just under an hour ago overlayed against a topography map that was made from the pass of another drone with ground penetrating radar. It showed cavernous areas within the rock that could be caves.

All below appeared quiet. Jackson again gazed at the sky for a moment, admiring its beauty. Then his gaze swept the ground below them. He listened to the exchange through his headphones of BT and the pilot, discussing the best spot for the team to drop. They would rappel down from a low altitude.

Deciding on the location nestled in between three possible locations, the chopper moved to that position and dropped to the optimal altitude. The men slipped on their NVGs and secured their weapons for the descent. Jackson secured the rope and tossed its length through the open door. He was the first to descend leaving Roth at the door, his weapon trained on the rugged terrain below.

Jackson landed on some loose rock that slid as his boots made contact. It was a good thing he still had a tight grip on the rope, or he would have gone down. He transmitted the condition to the others, so they'd be careful. Then he stepped away and held his M4 at the ready, covering the area.

Roth was the next to descend. More of the ground slipped out from beneath him. "Oh, hell, the rocks are loose." He took up a cover position as well, facing the opposite direction.

BT came down next. He landed, his feet coming completely out from beneath him. Like the others, only his tight hold on the rope kept him from sliding down the steep embankment. When he'd steadied himself on his feet, only then did he release the rope.

He took a step towards Jackson and the earth gave way, his feet sliding with the loose rocks. He was on his side, plummeting down the rock face a second later. He managed to reacquire the very edge of the rope with his left hand, but the angle in which he did, twisted his wrist into an unnatural, painful position. And when the line went taught and his sliding stopped, it did so with a jerk, and he felt something snap in his wrist. The pain was horrendous, but he still held on knowing he'd slide hundreds of feet down the mountain if he didn't.

"BT's down. Hold on your descent, Bubbles," Roth broadcast as he carefully moved to a position where he could see how far over the edge he'd gone. "Hold on, BT. We'll come to get you."

By this time, Jackson had reached the side of the embankment and stood beside Roth. Jackson deployed a rope and tied himself off to a sturdy nearby tree. Roth wrapped the rope around himself to hold it as a backup and Jackson rappelled down a few feet to the right of where BT dangled. The steep grade of the rock wall slipped away each time his boots made contact with it.

Once he was beside BT, he side-stepped to reach him. He clamped his own line to secure himself, and then tied a line to his downed teammate. He noticed the very unnatural position BT's left wrist was twisted into under the rope. His right hand also grasped the rope but that left hand's position looked bad. If it wasn't broken, tendons and ligaments were surely torn.

Jackson and Roth helped to pull BT up, who walked up the face of the mountain as the two others pulled him up. When he reached the top and got over to a spot with better footing, Roth examined the wrist. He was sure it was broken. BT didn't argue with that assessment. Roth splinted it. Then, they had Michael lower a lift, and BT was hoisted back aboard the aircraft, much to his grumbling to the contrary. He'd reopen his tablet and direct the team from an overwatch position. Michael helped him onboard before he took hold of the rope to go down. Jackson stood at the bottom and helped to guide Michael to find sure footing as he landed from his descent.

The three men continued towards the first location they would investigate. It was not ideal operating with only the three of them on the ground, but it was necessary. They were there. They couldn't call it off now. Besides, they were covered. Yvette and Smith were on line at HQ, as were the four members of Alpha Team. Everyone was aware of their situation. HQ was watching their area closely from a satellite that had been dedicated to the area.

The three men spent the next six hours hiking through the very rocky landscape, which often required the use of a rope to climb to traverse the topography rather than hiking for miles to make their way around the mountains on trails and dirt roads. They checked out three locations that could have hidden caves where the people they sought could have been. Nothing.

Through comms, BT transmitted information on the next site. This one he felt held promise. A new drone pass showed multiple heat signatures less than an hour before. It was nearly twenty-four hundred hours. Unless it was a heard of animals, who would be moving around the mountain at nearly midnight? More than likely military rather than civilians.

Oscar

Through night vision binoculars, Jackson focused on the area where the drone had picked up heat signatures. They were on a ridge overlooking the densely wooded area below where significant movement was taking place. They knew the mouth of a cave was also there. There were at least a dozen heat signatures in the immediate area, and they weren't animals. He couldn't get a good enough look through the branches and leaves to determine who he was looking at.

"We need to move in closer," Jackson broadcast.

"Negative, Jax, hold position. Alpha is moving in on your location as backup," Yvette transmitted from HQ.

"What's the ETA?" Jackson asked.

"Thirty minutes."

"As long as they don't leave the area, we'll hold position. We're going to move in just a touch closer, but we'll maintain a safe distance," Jackson broadcast.

"Roger that, Jax. We're watching the area," Yvette replied.

"Thank you, Control."

The three men covered each other moving slowly and noiselessly down the hill. They kept the target area in sight. It wasn't until they were two-thirds of the way down the steep hill that they could determine with certainty that there were men who looked like villagers in addition to men in green and beige camouflage, carrying weapons, who could only be military. There didn't seem to be any animosity between them. Though they didn't understand the language the men spoke, they appeared to converse cordially.

They held position and observed. Men who they believed to be villagers walked around freely, into the mouth of the cave, into the nearby woods on the other side of the little valley they were in. They didn't seem to be patrolling. Roth theorized they went into those woods to take a piss. It sounded as good as any other theory as to what they were doing over that way to Jackson and Michael.

"You've got an incoming Jeep from the west, Echo. We've got four heat signatures. Alpha Team's ETA is five minutes," Yvette broadcast. "Any sight of our missionaries?"

"Negative, Control. No white faces among those we've seen," Jackson replied. "No women or children either."

"We're coming in from your south, Echo," Cooper's voice came through the men's comms. "How many Tangos you got?"

"I've counting about ten armed and in uniform, Coop," Jackson said.

From the west side of the gathering spot below, a shout spurred the congregation of men into action. Those not in uniform disappeared into the mouth of the cave. Those with weapons took up a position so that they aimed into the small clearing which very well could have led to the road. It surely was the only place drivable in the immediate vicinity.

"Something's happening," Roth whispered into his comms. "We've got movement indicating they're taking a defensive posture."

"That Jeep is nearly on top of you," Yvette said.

"Affirmative, we have it in sight," Cooper said. "Four heavily armed men, and I mean heavily armed. Alpha is moving to take up cover positions. This feels like they're about to attack."

"But which side do we support?" Roth asked.

"We stay out of it for as long as we can,"

Cooper replied.

"We should know by what we observe who are the bad guys in play," Garcia added.

Madison hunkered down a few feet from Cooper. They exchanged glances and meaningful head nods. Then they both affixed their gazes through their scopes to watch the carnage play out.

The Jeep came in fast, the man in the front passenger seat firing his weapon on full-automatic. He hit at least half of the men on the ground. As they took return fire from those left on the ground, one of the men in the back fired an RPG, which exploded with a boiling fireball where the men had been in front of the mouth of the cave. What remained was a charred mess. A few more men in camouflage with weapons took up position at the mouth of the cave and returned fire, hitting the driver. The Jeep careened to the right and plowed into a tree, expelling the occupants like rag dolls.

None of the Shepherd Security personnel could tell the difference between the two forces. Their uniforms looked similar, though from the distance they were from the Tangos, they could not see identifying insignia on their uniforms, if there was any.

From the men near the cave and from

within, there was shouting and several of the men who looked like villagers ran from the cave and over to where the Jeep crashed. One of the men from the Jeep lay near it. He was writhing in pain. One of the villagers who ran to him, picked up a rock and repeatedly bashed his head in until he was convinced the man was no longer alive. The others gathered their weapons and other supplies from the Jeep. Then they scurried back to the cave.

"What the hell?" Doc voiced for the team, watching this play out.

"You've got more company," Yvette's voice came. "Half a click to your west, on foot. They must have come out of a cave as they weren't there and now, they are, about a dozen."

"Fuck," Garcia growled. "They're coming up behind us."

They couldn't go to the north as the steep grade would block them. Their only option was to circle far enough out to the south that they could cross the clearing far enough out of view of the cave opening. And they had to move fast without catching the attention of the men who were on alert, waiting for another attack.

Jackson, Roth, and Michael kept their weapons trained on the men near the cave, ready to lay down cover fire if they detected Alpha Team. Through comms, Yvette provided a narrative of the proximity of the twelve-man force approaching from the west. They were heading right for them. Everyone knew that when they arrived, all hell would break loose. And at that moment, it wouldn't matter who was who, RSF or SAF. The Shepherd Security Team only cared about civilians, which it appeared were in the cave. Male villagers anyway. But where were the women and children and the American Missionaries?

Papa

"The Tangos are within one hundred yards of you," Yvette announced. "They've split. Six are holding position to the west, the other six are circling to the south right behind you, Alpha."

Every one of the Shepherd Security Team knew that meant one thing. This force was setting up for a major offensive against those in front of and in the cave. "Echo, cover the cave and the force to the west. Alpha will handle the incoming behind us."

"Roger, that, Coop," Jackson replied.

In the helicopter, which circled far enough away to not be seen or heard, BT was frustrated hearing the events play out and the fact that he was sidelined. He knew that Alpha Team and Roth could handle themselves, but Michael had no experience with this type of mission. He didn't have time to ponder it any further as the assault immediately took place.

Shattering the serene area, deafening gunfire suddenly exploded along with a grenade in front of the cave. It was too far away from the men to do any damage to them. Someone missed their target. It was a costly mistake. Return fire tore through the brush where the grenade had originated. Sounds indicating men had been shot drifted out rather than more bullets answering the volley.

That was when the men who'd come up behind Alpha Team opened fire at the men, now showing themselves at the mouth of the cave. The bright bursts from their AK-47s lit up the tree line, giving their position up. They cut down the men in front of the cave. They moved forward, leaving the safety of the tree line behind them.

It was then that one of them saw Alpha Team, crouching down for cover behind brush and tree stumps. He called out in their native language as he swung the barrel of his rifle towards Alpha Team's position. Alpha Team reacted fast and fired at the six men, neutralizing the threat they posed.

"I have two retreating to the west," Yvette transmitted. "It looks like everyone else has been neutralized, but you're going to want to check them to be sure."

Shepherd Security would let them go. Now they turned their attention to the cave. No one looked alive in front of it. They waited a few minutes. No movement. Alpha Team circled and confirmed the casualties.

"I wish they would have issued us that anticholinergic laden device," Garcia lamented. "Now would be a good time to use it to breach that cave." They'd made the request, and it had been declined.

"We could still pop a few flash bangs in and see what happens," Cooper said.

"Or we could try calling out in English and see if our American Missionaries answer," Michael suggested.

Cooper chuckled. "Jax and Roth, move into position along the east side of the cave opening and be ready to deploy flash bangs. Garcia and I will do the same on the west side. We'll call in, speaking English first. If there's no answer, we toss in the flash bangs."

"I'd like to try to speak to them in Arabic. I know Sudanese Arabic is different than what I speak, but there may be enough commonality that they understand a little of what I'm saying," Madison said.

Cooper stared at his wife for a moment. He'd prefer she remain in the semi-safety of the tree line, but she was right. "Approved. Xena will approach with Garcia and me."

Moving stealthily through the pre-dawn night, they all got into position.

"You in the cave! We're the American military here to rescue the missionaries and the people of that village that was attacked. Reply!" Cooper yelled. He nodded to Madison.

She called in a similar message but added the question asking if there were women and children inside. They waited a few beats and heard nothing. Not even the sounds of movement.

"One last time, if there are any Americans in the cave, we're here to rescue you!" Cooper called again.

He gave it thirty seconds. "Be prepared to deploy flash bangs in five, four, three," he counted down.

"Yes, we're here!" a male voice with a distinct Texas accent called back.

"We have an American," Cooper transmitted. "Stand down." Then he raised his voice and called back into the cave. "We need you all to come out with your hands up. The threat out here is neutralized."

One by one they came out of the cave. The five American missionaries, all white men, carrying local village children. The other women and children came out behind them followed by the village's men and five men in uniform. They were unarmed.

Quebec

Friday, December 22

Angel arrived at her desk at nine-thirty after once again dropping off Sammy and Hahna at school before coming into work. It was the last day of school for the kids before the Christmas break. She would only be at the office for an hour to take care of a few things. There was a Christmas party at school that all the parents of the kids in the class were invited to. She appreciated the flexibility that Shepherd gave her to balance the kids and her job. She didn't want to miss Sammy's first school Christmas party. She'd even left Johanna with Elizabeth so she could focus on Sammy while she was there.

She checked the staff calendar as she logged herself as 'in'. She noticed that Bravo Team was in the office and further investigating Shepherd's calendar, she saw that they had been in a meeting with him for the last hour. Not many meetings lasted an hour. Shepherd believed in direct and to the point.

She'd only met the men on Bravo Team a handful of times. She made their travel arrangements and had some interaction with them over the years, so she could say they weren't complete strangers. Jackson had worked with them and spoke highly of them. But she didn't know them well. That would soon change, she was sure.

Inside Shepherd's office the five men sat on the leather couches and chairs to the side of the conference table. This was the first time in over a year that all four members of Bravo Team were at HQ with Shepherd. Shepherd had regular video meetings with the team and team lead Tommy 'Louisa' Flores had come in over Thanksgiving to coordinate a few of the details of the team returning to HQ. In the hour the five of them had been meeting, not only had it been a comfortable homecoming, but they'd covered a lot too.

All four members of Bravo Team were appreciative that Shepherd had Angel make the reservations at the local extended stay hotel giving them their own rooms. Even though while handling their security gigs they only had two rooms, they would typically work two men on, two men off during a twenty-four-hour period, so each man had a room to himself while his roommate worked. Shepherd of course knew this. That was one of the reasons he'd had Angel make the reservations as he had.

Additionally, each man had a storage locker of all their belongings including their vehicles stored in a separate portion of the private Shepherd Security garage area. Shepherd had Requisition Ryan tend to all four vehicles to ensure they were in working order, gassed up, and available to their owners. He had even moved them into the main agency garage for them the day before they were due. They appreciated that gesture also.

"Shep, I speak for the team when I say we only have maybe five years left in us before we'll be thinking about retirement. That'll put us all at around thirty years in. We'll each draw nice retirement pay to live comfortably on," Tommy Flores said. "I've been saving and have my eye on a horse farm in Texas."

"I can appreciate that," Shepherd said. "We'd talked briefly around that topic before. What it comes down to is what do you see these last five years of your career looking like? Continuing with the private security gigs wasn't it."

"We've talked about this amongst ourselves, Shep," Tommy began, "and if it's not too disrespectful to put it out there, none of us are up for a return to the Sandbox or Africa unless American's are in a dire emergency situation and there is no one else who can go get them. Messing with the cartel drug fucks who have no regard for human life isn't on the top of our list either, but we know the illegal drugs and those cartel fucks are a serious risk to Americans, so avoiding those types of cases isn't possible. We are interested in the agency's new CIA Referral Cases, and we're all more than qualified to staff Ops. When we spoke over Thanksgiving, you mentioned the possibility of creating a new arm of the agency for local investigations. We'd like to discuss that further."

Shepherd felt his irritation build. Yes, they'd talked about that possibility, but he'd made it clear it was months away before it would be talked about seriously. "Tommy, you know that drugs are the number one threat domestically to American lives right now, so those cases will continue to dominate the cases the agency works."

"If I wanted to go after cartel fucks, I'd have joined the DEA," Tommy argued, his dark eyes focused on Shepherd. They went way back. He knew he could talk openly with his boss. "The whole war on drugs has been a losing proposition since that war was declared. We both know it's supply and demand and as long as there is demand, there will be supply."

"Shep, my problem with the DEA cases is the travel. If I'd wanted to stay on the road every week, I would have lobbied to continue the private security contract," Navy SEAL Eddie 'Needles' Winston, M.D. said. "We're burned out from two years on the road protecting for the most part, entitled assholes who had little appreciation for the job we were doing. As you know, many of them fought the protection we put in place."

"You did a good job. You made a good name for this agency as a private security firm. It had never been the plan to leave you on that job as long as we did. I can appreciate your desire to stay in one place for a while but for almost all of our work, travel is a requirement."

"Almost all," Eddie repeated. "What about the slice of that work that isn't included in that statement?"

Marine Raider Elijah 'Kegger' Robinson laughed, his white teeth a contrast to his dark skin with laugh lines bracketing his eyes and lips. "Young bucks, let them have the action. I'm decent with a screwdriver. I wouldn't mind doing a few of those PGP installs every month, but a steady diet of the travel isn't appealing right now."

"I could use you there. I have several members of that team who do want to work the cases you don't," Shepherd said.

Elijah laughed again. "Those young bucks."

Shepherd nodded. "We were all the same when we were younger, eager, and cocky. Hell, doesn't seem that long ago, but it was."

"And now look at you, a married man," Elijah joked. "Who would have guessed that?"

Shepherd laughed. "I'm sorry that job ran over, and you couldn't come to the wedding."

"Us too. We'd have liked to have been there. There's no doubt this agency has changed a lot over the last two years," Tommy said. "You and half the men are married, and some have kids. I'm sure it's going to feel like a foreign landscape to us for a while."

"We've implemented a rotation to give the men with families more time at HQ. They're averaging fifty percent home, fifty percent away and it's working for them," Shepherd said. "It comes down to the work though and where the jobs are. I'm aware of the time on the road Bravo Team has logged. I've already scheduled you to be at HQ for the entire month of January. That should also get you re-acclimated to the agency environment."

"If I can make a pitch," former Green Beret Kenny 'Ducky' Gallup spoke up. "I would be happy working Ops overnights for the month. If I remember correctly, that had always been a hard shift to fill, but I've been on mostly overnights for the last two years. Switching to regular day shifts isn't going to be easy."

"I can honor that request for most of the

month," Shepherd said. "There is some training we'll have scheduled as part of that re-acclimation we talked about. Cooper will schedule that with you when the team gets back."

"That must have been a hell of an ask from the DoD for you to send all four teams. We haven't all operated together since you were shot," Gallup said.

"I wasn't crazy about leaving HQ and all the families unprotected, but I have staff at HQ that could handle things if anything went down, me included. The job in Africa was important. And I didn't think it could be done safely with fewer boots on the ground than I sent."

"Had we already been checked in; would you have sent us?" Tommy asked.

"This month, no. You've been out of the mindset needed for that job for too long. After you'd been here for a few months and I knew your skills and instincts were still up to snuff, probably. I would have had to evaluate all cases and personnel assignments when the request came for that job."

"So, what does our next thirty days look like?" Tommy asked.

"Training and getting acquainted with the new team members. You will each do a few shifts in Ops to re-familiarize yourselves with how we do things. Attendance at our Christmas Eve dinner with the team and their families and at Lambchop and Michaela's wedding is mandatory."

The four men nodded.

"But from the twenty-fifth to the thirtieth, you're all on leave," Shepherd said.

"Fair enough," Tommy said. "Anything else?"

"No, settle into your new offices, schedule face to face meetings with Lassiter within the next few days, and pop into Ops to see Yvette and Dupont. They're on this morning. Gallup, you can work out a schedule with her for an overnight Ops shift before leave time starts."

Knowing they'd just been dismissed the four men stood. Shepherd did as well. He reached his hand to shake each of the men's hands. "Welcome back. I'm sure we can make schedules for you each that you'll find acceptable."

"We're sure you can too, or we would have just put in our retirement papers. We're not quite ready for that yet, though," Tommy said.

"I'm glad," Shepherd said.

The four men filed out and headed towards Angel's desk, hoping to find her there.

Romeo

Angel touched base with Dahlia to ensure she would be in by ten thirty to cover the reception desk. Angel was so excited to go to the Christmas party at Sammy's school. She wished Jackson was home so he could have gone as well. It was only an hour long, but it was one of those things she wouldn't miss. She was sad Jackson would.

To make the day special for Sammy, she planned to take him out to lunch, just the two of them, a mom and son lunch date. Then in the afternoon, the two of them would go to Elizabeth's house and she would babysit while Elizabeth went to Hahna's class Christmas party. She knew that Madison was bummed that she couldn't be there. Elizabeth was a second mother to Hahna, so of course she would be there, probably would even if Madison had been in town.

"Hello, Beautiful," Tommy greeted Angel, coming up behind her.

Angel smiled as she stood. "Hello. I saw you were in with Shepherd." She embraced each man while personally greeting him by name. "It's nice to see you again so soon, Tommy."

"Always my pleasure," Tommy said.

"Kenny, it's been a while," she said. She noticed his temples had gotten just a touch of gray since she'd seen him last. His jet-black hair had always been free of the signs of aging. His face too had gotten a few creases making him look closer to his age than he had previously.

"You look good, Angel. I'm glad life is treating you well," Kenny said.

"Hello Elijah," she said giving him a hug. His black hair was solid gray now, including his beard and mustache. His smile was as easy to come as she remembered.

"Hello, Angel. It's nice to see you. I can't wait to lift a beer with that husband of yours."

"I know he'll enjoy that," she said. Then she embraced Eddie. "I'm glad you will all be here at HQ through January. Did you get checked into the extended stay hotel okay?" she asked them all.

"Yes, thank you. As always, you handled all our arrangements with no issue," Eddie said.

Eddie had turned gray prematurely in his thirties. He was one of those men who looked distinguished with the gray hair, much like how she thought an older Sean Connery looked sexier than the younger version. "Good, glad to hear that."

"Where are the kids?" Elijah asked. "I heard you brought them to work with you."

"On some days. Sammy is in preschool now, three mornings a week."

"Damn, he's old enough for that?" Eddie said.

"Yes, he is," Angel said with a smile. "I'm sure you know, but if you need anything, let me know."

"Thanks, Angel," Elijah said, his hand on her shoulder.

"We better go find our offices and poke our heads into Ops," Tommy said. "We'll catch you later."

"I'll be leaving for the day in less than an hour. Dahlia will be filling in for me. She'll order lunch and let everyone know when it's here. I was just messaging her to remind her that Bravo Team is in today, so she'll remember to notify you."

"Remind me again who Dahlia is?" Kenny asked.

"Michael Cooper's girlfriend, and Brielle Sherman's sister. Brielle, who's married to the Birdman," Angel clarified.

"Oh, that's right," Kenny said. "I've talked to Brielle a couple times. It'll be nice to meet her."

Sierra

Bravo Team's next stop was Ops. This was the team the men of Bravo had worked the most closely with over the past two years. Yvette and Dupont were on duty. They all knew them both well from before their private security gig.

"Hey Beautiful," Tommy greeted Yvette.

"Louisa, you shameless flirt!" Yvette replied as she stood. She embraced him. "How the hell are you?"

"Better now that I've seen you," he said with a smile and a wink.

The reunion and banter between the six of them continued, including Yvette pointing out to Ducky how much gray was showing at his temples. She also teased Kegger about losing his razor. Needles, she remarked looked as suave as always.

"I'm suave," Eddie 'Needles' said with an attitude flung at Kenny and Elijah.

"Fuck you," Elijah said with a smile while his hand rubbed his unshaven face. "This is a disguise that has helped me blend in."

Dupont laughed. "Only if you're trying to pass as homeless, Kegger."

"Well, at my age, I don't have to give a shit any longer," Elijah, the accomplished Marine Raider said.

"They call that being an old fuck, these days," Kenny, the Green Beret pointed out.

"You're right up there with me," Elijah told Kenny.

"Yeah, but I don't look it." He laughed.

"Seriously, guys, glad you're back with us," Yvette said.

"Things sure seemed to have changed around here," Tommy said. "We know there will be a lot of new faces. Hell, I'd just gotten used to Angel being on board, but now she told us there is another receptionist who fills in for her that we've got to get used to."

"There's actually a few," Yvette said. "Shepherd hiring the other wives and girlfriends works well, keeps our circle small and it lets Angel balance her time with work and her family. Shepherd allows her and Brielle both to work from home half the week."

"I think Shepherd's getting soft in his old age," Kenny said.

"I won't tell him you said that," Dupont said with a laugh. "He's smart, knows how to help his people do a good job."

"He's always been smart, has always known how to enable his people to do their best," Kenny agreed.

"So, Shepherd told us you boys will all be rotated in after January for some shifts here in Ops," Yvette said. "Will seem like old times."

"Looking forward to it, Red," Elijah said.

"I've been pulling overnights," Kenny said. "I'd prefer to stay on them for now." His gaze shifted to Dupont. "Don't you normally prefer them too?"

"Yeah. I'm sure we'll pull some shifts together." He smiled and nodded. "And then we can properly catch up."

"I look forward to it," Kenny said.

Just then, Laura Lee let herself back into Ops, surprised by the four men inside that hadn't been there when she'd left an hour earlier, and who she recognized, but couldn't name. "Oh, hello," she said, her eyes sweeping over the men.

"Hello, Beautiful," Tommy said. "I believe you are Lieutenant Laura Lee Saxton."

Her surprised gaze went to Brad. "Yes, I am."

Tommy Flores laughed. "I'm Flores, Louisa."

"Oh, Bravo Team," Laura Lee said. "It's nice to meet you. I've heard a lot about you four."

"Don't believe any of it," Kenny said.

"Hello Laura," Elijah greeted her. "Army Corps of Engineers. That's impressive."

Dupont placed his hands on her shoulders. "And now just about to complete full Operator training as well. She is impressive."

"Put your leg down, sonny," Elijah said. "I know the two of you are involved." He winked at Yvette. "A little birdy has kept us filled in on all the gossip around here. But for the life of me, I can't see Shepherd approving of all these intra-agency relationships. Hell, Michaela knocked up by Lambchop, way to go Lambchop, but Shepherd being okay with it?" He shook his head.

"There you go sounding like an old man again," Kenny teased him. "And you're just jealous that Lambchop got a date with her."

"Damn right I am," Elijah admitted.

The others all chuckled.

"None of the relationships interfere with agency business," Yvette said. "I think after Cooper and Madison got together, Shepherd realized he'd rather have them together than lose either one of them, and they make it work damn well."

Tango

Saturday, December 23rd

The flight back from Sudan was long. Waiting for their pilots, the layover at Ramstein Air Force Base lasted four hours. All sixteen members of the team were anxious to get home. BT had not told Evie about his broken wrist. He'd wait to do that in person. He'd sworn his teammates to secrecy regarding it. He didn't need any of their wives or girlfriends telling Evie before he could. At least it didn't require surgery. The upside would be that he'd staff Ops and be home for a few months.

As the plane touched down at O'Hare, excitement and a sense of relief washed over the team. They'd made it home for Christmas. Those with children especially felt it. Even the team members who had a significant other knew them being home would make their special person happy. They knew it was hard for a woman to be with them, the last-minute missions, the danger, the covert nature of the job.

They deplaned and quickly transferred their

gear to the four vehicles they'd left parked outside the hangar when they left just over a week earlier. It was thirteen hundred hours on Saturday, December twenty-third. The traffic was light on the drive back to the Shepherd Security building. They made it in a half hour. They'd have a short debrief with Shepherd before they could all head home.

The private parking garage was a welcome sight as the four vehicles pulled in and parked in front of the elevator and door into the building. BT planned to pop into Evie's vet clinic really quick after he'd stowed his gear and before the debrief. She was open until fifteen hundred hours. Given his broken wrist, he wouldn't help unload any of the heavier items. While the rest of the team did, he ran up the stairs to the ground floor.

He had text messaged Evie after they landed, to let her know he was back and would stop by the clinic before the debrief, so she was expecting him. He pushed through the public entrance to the clinic in the lobby. The exam room door was open and he could see her within with a patient, a lab mix and its owner, an older man who held it on the exam table.

Evie locked eyes with Brody and her smile instantly spread wider. "Can you excuse me for just a moment please?" she said to her patient's owner. She walked around him and came into her waiting room and embraced Brody. "I'm so glad you made it back," she whispered in his ear as she embraced him. "I missed you."

BT wrapped his arms around her and returned the hug. "I missed you too. I just wanted to see you really quick. I have a debrief but will be done before you close."

She pulled back and nodded, her eyes gazing deeply into his. "I love you, Brody."

"I love you too, Evie." He pulled his left arm with the black aircast wrist brace into sight. "I had a little accident. It's broken."

"Oh, my God, Brody. Are you okay?"

"Yes. I'm fine, sweetheart. And I'll be assigned to Ops for the next few months, so I'll be home. That's a plus." He smiled to reassure her.

"Are you in much pain?"

"Not much. I'll have to see an ortho soon. They didn't want to cast it until the swelling went down. We'll see, maybe the aircast will be all I need." He pressed a soft kiss to her frowning lips. "I have to go, and you have a patient. I'll tell you about it later, at home."

Evie nodded. "Okay, yeah. I'll see you after your meeting." She returned to her patient as BT left her office.

By the time BT made it to the conference

room, the others were all making their way there too. Once they were all present and seated, Cooper text messaged Shepherd to let him know they were ready. He'd been in his office with the door closed on a video call with his DoD contact.

"Sorry for making you wait," Shepherd said as he entered the conference room and closed the door. He took his seat. "But that call was important. Our team is now officially stood down from active with the DoD. From now until January first we will not be scrambled, no matter what goes down. If there is something that dire, they will contact me with a request that I can either approve or deny. It would have to be earthshattering for me to approve it as the team would be scattered to all points. After this meeting, consider yourselves all on leave until December thirty-first at one hundred hours."

The team smiled, some cheered, and voices overlapped with each other thanking Shepherd.

"Good job on the Sudan mission," he continued. "And thank you for all getting your mission reports submitted. You all, once again, demonstrated proficiency with operating in foreign terrain while integrating with our active-duty forces. This is a key indicator of your professionalism and your superior level of training and dedication to the mission. The DoD thanks us for taking this one on. Even though the members of the missionary team decided to remain in Sudan, you got them, and the villagers delivered to a refugee camp where they will enjoy a Christmas free of worry of being attacked. This was a huge win."

"Were there any repercussions regarding the FSA members we had to neutralize?" Cooper asked.

"No. Nor should there be. That whole region is volatile and who is in control is constantly shifting," Shepherd replied. "Unfortunately, that village will not be the last one that will be attacked."

"I just hope it's the last we'll be sent to," Lambchop said. "Even though no one has said it, we all know they were targeted because they are Christians."

Shepherd frowned and nodded. "The instability of the region does have religious aspects driving it. This isn't our fight and had the American's not been amongst the missing from that village, we never would have gone in. I agree with you, Lambchop, hopefully it will be the last we're involved in that conflict."

"Amen," Lambchop said.

"Okay, that's it. I'll see all of you at sixteen hundred tomorrow for our Christmas Eve festivities. Bravo Team checked in yesterday and they will be there. Angel and the planners of the event did a wonderful job as always."

The mood was light and relaxed as all the team members stood and then filed out of the conference room. They were stood down and officially on leave. Cooper, Jackson, and Garcia would take shifts in Ops to help out. Ops still had to be manned, and the team and their families still needed to be watched over.

Uniform

On his way home from the office, Sloan stopped at the grocery store. He bought a bottle of champagne and a bouquet of flowers for Kaylee. His heart soared with excitement when he called to let her know the team was heading home and she told him she was pregnant. But his heart clenched in his chest to hear the fear in her voice of another miscarriage. It loomed over her, clouding her happiness. He knew he had to do something to ease her fears.

He came through the door from the garage to find her curled up on the couch under a blanket sleeping. After he set his backpack down and placed the bottle of champagne on the kitchen table, he brought the bouquet of flowers with him to the couch. He knelt in front of her and gently placed a hand on her shoulder. "Kaylee, are you okay?" He pressed a kiss to her forehead.

Kaylee came awake, feeling Gary's touch and hearing his voice. When she opened her eyes, he was kneeling in front of her. "Hi. I'm glad you're home." She smiled. "I missed you."

He kissed her again. "Do you feel okay, babe?"

"Yes, just so tired."

"Didn't you sleep well last night?" He was concerned.

"I'm having a lot of nausea. My stomach was upset all night."

"That's a good sign of a healthy pregnancy, isn't it?" he asked.

"That's what they say." She sat up. That was when she saw the flowers. "Oh, Gary, they're beautiful." He presented them to her, and she teared up. He was the sweetest man. She was so lucky that they had this second chance for a life together.

"Kaylee, what's the matter? You're crying."

"Damned pregnancy hormones," she said. "I've been so emotional the last few weeks. And I just pray that I carry this one to term."

He embraced her. "No negative thoughts, whatsoever, you got it? You're pregnant and we are having a baby. We won't even consider the possibility of a miscarriage. Lightning is not going to strike twice. I have a feeling about this Kaylee. And it's a strong feeling that everything will be okay."

She embraced him and held on, held onto

his confidence. "I love you and we'll face whatever will come together."

"Yes, together, baby. I love you."

***

Cooper and Madison gave Doc a lift back to his place so they could pick Hahna up. After the debrief Doc called Elizabeth to let her know they'd be heading home within a few minutes to ensure she'd be there. When they'd landed at O'Hare, Madison had text messaged her to let her know they'd be there to get Hahna as soon as they could.

Madison missed that little girl like crazy when she was away on a mission. From the moment she'd picked her up and held her, she knew she could never let her go. The trust in Hahna's eyes that day when they latched on to hers, did something to Madison's heart. She knew Cooper didn't understand it right away, but it didn't take long for him to understand the instant bond that had been formed.

As he formed his own fatherly bond with Hahna, he knew he'd been changed. As she got more comfortable with them and her new life in America, he saw this incredible spirit in his adoptive daughter that warmed his heart. Her personality was sweet, despite what she'd been through. And he fell even more deeply in love with Madison watching her be a mother to that little girl.

They pulled into Doc and Elizabeth's driveway. Doc pulled his bags from the back of the SUV and then the three of them walked to the front door. Knowing Olivia could be down for a nap, they entered quietly to find Elizabeth and Hahna snuggled under a blanket on the couch watching The Polar Express. By the looks of it, it was nearly over. Olivia was asleep on Elizabeth's lap.

"Mommy! Daddy! Uncle Doc!" Hahna squealed and then jumped up. She crawled over the arm of the couch to run to them. Madison and Cooper gave her a hug at the same time, what they referred to as a Cooper family group hug. It was Hahna's favorite to be smooshed between the two of them. Then Hahna gave Doc a hug too.

Elizabeth laid Olivia onto the couch, who slept through the homecoming, and she embraced Doc and held him tightly. "I'm glad you're home. I missed you," she whispered into his ear.

"I love you, honey," he whispered back. He kissed her lips.

Then Elizabeth bent down to Hahna and gave her a hug and a kiss. "I'll see you tomorrow at the Christmas Eve party. Make sure you show your mommy and daddy everything in your backpack from your school party yesterday."

"Auntie Elizabeth made a video for you,"

Hahna said, her face directed to Madison and Cooper.

"That was wonderful of Auntie Elizabeth to do that for us. We were so sorry work ran over and we couldn't be there," Madison said.

"That's okay, Mommy," Hahna said. "Next year. And I'll be better singing the Christmas songs then too."

Madison embraced her again. "I'm sure you were wonderful this year. I can't wait to watch Auntie Elizabeth's video."

Elizabeth tapped on her phone. "Just sent it to you."

Madison gave Elizabeth a hug before they left. "Thank you for being there for her, as always."

"I love her as much as you do," Elizabeth said. "She's one lucky little girl that four of us love her so much. Some children don't get even one set of loving parents, but she has two."

Doc wrapped his arm around Elizabeth. "She deserves it," he said. He'd been there when they found Hahna in the deplorable conditions that no person, let alone a little child, should be in. All of Alpha, Delta, and Charlie were on that mission. It was one of those missions that stuck with them and changed them.

Victor

Christmas Eve

Angel arrived at the Shepherd Security Building an hour before the holiday party was to begin. Johanna was down for her afternoon nap and Sammy was having a quiet time. Jackson would bring them at four. Diana, Kaylee and Sloan, and Dahlia and Michael were already in the rec room setting up when she entered the room.

"Merry Christmas, everyone," she greeted as she entered. They all responded in kind. "Wow, you've already got so much done."

The tables and chairs were all set up in neat rows. Two tables were set up for the buffet area for the food to be set out, so lines could go around both sides to speed along the partygoers serving their food. Another table was set up that would house the self-serve bar. Sparkling water, sodas, wine, and beer would be on offer. They even had tablecloths spread over each table.

Her gaze went to the large Christmas Tree on the far wall and the sea of gifts that flowed out into the room from beneath it. Many more gifts were there now than had been under it when she was last in the office on Friday. Each adult had one gift from Shepherd and the agency that she had picked out. For the kids, there were many gifts for each of them.

Angel got busy and plugged in all the lit decorations, lights, garland, and a few animated figures. She also started the Christmas music that would welcome the guests as they entered. It would play softly in the background of the room and out in the hallway, and she'd turn it off as the noise in the room made it impossible to hear. But it would set the initial mood.

When the caterers called her to say that they'd arrived with the food, Angel, Sloan, and Michael went down in the public elevator to the ground floor with a cart to get the food. The aroma in the elevator on the way back up made Angel's stomach growl with hunger. It all smelled so good.

By the time they brought the food into the rec room, the others had started to arrive. The room filled up fast after that. As Ops still needed to be manned, several team members volunteered to take one-hour shifts during the party, including Shepherd. The party would be over around twenty-two hundred. Yvette and Miraldi would cover Ops overnight.

That evening and the next morning,

Christmas Day, would be busy for Ops logging each team member's travel plans.

Immediately after the party ended, Laura Lee Saxton, Dupont, and Burke would drive to O'Hare Airport together to fly to Richmond, Virginia to spend Christmas morning and a few days with her family. Dupont and Laura Lee would get his car from the shop in Richmond that had repaired it and drive it to see his mother in North Carolina. They would drive home from there. Burke would fly back on the thirtieth.

The three other members of Charlie Team were all traveling as well. Mike Rogers' family lived in Denver. His flight left at zero six hundred the next morning. Jimmy Wilson and Carter Tessman were flying to Saint Thomas, in the U.S. Virgin Islands for a scuba diving and beach vacation. They would return on the thirtieth as well.

Mother and Annaka also had reservations to fly out that evening. Their destination was his family home in San Jose, California. They were both excited that they would wake up on Christmas morning with his family, who had accepted Annaka the second they heard about her. Because she had to be back on the twenty-eighth for her job at the Shedd Aquarium, they would fly home on the red eye on the twenty-seventh. It would be a quick trip, but they both appreciated they could spend Christmas with his family.

Doc, Elizabeth, and Olivia would fly to Houston to be with his family the next morning. He was the only member of Alpha Team that was traveling for the holiday. Jackson's sister and her family would arrive at their house on the twenty-sixth and stay for a few days. Madison's parents would arrive on Christmas Day in time for dinner. Her sister, Megan, had gotten a job at the airport and had to work the entire week, including Christmas Day, so she wouldn't be in. And of course, Garcia and Sienna would not travel. They had no family that either were in contact with. They would enjoy Christmas Day with Angel and Jackson's little family.

Sloan and Kaylee would fly to Cleveland to be with both their families on Christmas morning. They decided they wouldn't share the news of her pregnancy with anyone else until she passed the twelve-week mark. She had an appointment with the OB, Doctor Norman, on Friday, the twenty-ninth. They would fly home the day before.

Brielle and Brian Sherman were excited to celebrate their first Christmas with their son at home. They would host Dahlia and Michael, and Lambchop and Michaela for a home-cooked dinner on Christmas Day where they'd exchange presents. Michael and Dahlia would first enjoy a Christmas morning brunch at his brother and Madison's house. Dahlia had gone overboard buying gifts for everyone, but she'd had so much fun shopping.

Michaela's brother, Gregor, and his family were due in on the twenty-ninth. He and his wife, Catherine, had reconciled. Michaela and Gregor had become close since their father's death. They talked weekly and Michaela could say she was genuinely happy that Gregor would be at the wedding to walk her down the aisle as her father had wanted.

Lambchop's family of course lived locally. He and Michaela would enjoy a Christmas morning brunch with his parents, nephew, and nieces before they went over to the Sherman's house. His older sister, Faith, would fly in for their wedding, but couldn't make it for Christmas. Her husband was a doctor and on call, so he would not be able to be there. They were thrilled that they would get to spend time with Faith though.

Doctor Lassiter and his family had traveled out of town to spend Christmas with his wife's family. They'd be back in town by New Year's Eve, and he would be at the wedding. As he kept the family and the team separate, his wife would not attend with him.

Originally, Caleb Smith planned to go to Michigan with Hollyn to visit her family for Christmas. They had gone for Thanksgiving and brought his father with them. They had a wonderful time. But her family surprised them by planning to come to Chicago for Christmas.

Shepherd and Diana were hosting. Hollyn, Smith, and Smith's father were all invited. Smith would admit that he was a bit nervous about having Christmas dinner in his boss' home. But he was, after all, Hollyn's uncle now, and Smith knew he had to get over it. He was sure this was the first of many holidays they would spend together.

BT and Evie would remain at home for the holiday. Her veterinary clinic would be open between Christmas and the New Year. They looked forward to their first Christmas together to start building their new traditions. Sebastian Roth would drive to Indianapolis first thing in the morning to spend Christmas with his mother and sister. Living so close to his mother was a perk of working for Shepherd Security. He'd been able to visit with her more times in the last year than in the last five.

Whiskey

As the Christmas Eve festivities got underway, the chaos in the room was music to Angel's ears. Based on the smiles she saw on everyone's faces, she judged they felt the same way. They each may have their own families, but this group, this Shepherd Security family, was important to each of them.

The four men of Bravo Team enjoyed reunions with members of the other teams they had not spent much time with over the past few years. The introductions to the significant others in their lives and their children kept the conversations going. Yvette knew they felt like the odd men out, but she also knew that they would be drawn right back into the team environment once they got acquainted or reacquainted with everyone.

At seventeen hundred, Cooper yelled above the many conversations, "Atten hut!"

The service members immediately came to attention. Their family's quieted.

"If you would all find a seat for dinner, please," Shepherd said. He and Diana had staked out their spot at one of the tables, which many of the others had as well. He raised his glass once everyone was seated. "Tonight, we celebrate a very special time together. This group, this family, is special. I thank each of you for your dedication and your sacrifice for the job we do. For the families, your support of your loved one who does this job is invaluable. Without you doing what you do at home, they would not be able to perform as they do. What this agency does is important and every single person in this room is vital to ensure we complete our missions at the high levels we do. I'm glad that we can pause today and for the next week for us to all celebrate Christmas together and with our families and friends over the next week. Diana and I wish you all a very Merry Christmas. To all of you!" He raised his glass a bit higher and then took a drink.

"Merry Christmas," in response in a jumble of voices replied. Everyone drank to his toast.

Lambchop stood next. "Tonight is indeed a special night. Tonight is the eve of our Lord and Savior's birth. We remember the events in Bethlehem that wonderful night. We've all heard the Bible stories of Joseph and Mary's trek to return to Bethlehem for the census. And with no room at any inn, they were forced to bed down in a stable, where Mary gave birth. That child was laid in a manger. That child, the King of Kings, brought many from foreign lands as they followed a star that burned brightly in the sky. They did so to honor him and bring him gifts. That child was of course, Jesus. We sing many Christmas songs about that blessed event. And our tradition of giving gifts is in remembrance of those gifts that were brought to baby Jesus that day."

He paused and his gaze shifted to the Christmas Tree which had many gifts around it as a big smile spread across his face. The others' gazes followed his and a quiet chuckle resounded through the room.

"As we enjoy this wonderful meal, may you each feel the presence of Jesus in your heart. Father, God, thank you for the bounty of this meal we will enjoy. Thank you for the people we share it with, the people in our lives who bring meaning to our existence. We are blessed with the wealth of family and friends, of teammates and colleagues. We are blessed with a purpose to serve others, to protect others as only we can. Father, may all here tonight feel joy as we celebrate Your Son's birth. Amen and Merry Christmas to each of you."

Everyone responded with either 'Amen', or 'Merry Christmas'.

Then Cooper stood. "One last toast, if I may." He raised his glass. "To Shepherd for hosting this dinner and party this evening. Thank you for all that you do for us. It's not hard for us to bring our best to the job when we know you have our backs."

"Here, here!" many voiced. There were claps, whoops, and hollers. Even Hahna and Sammy who didn't truly understand, cheered.

"Okay, the food is ready, let's let the families with kids get their plates first and then fall in and serve yourself. And thank you Shepherd and Angel for taking care of the dinner," Cooper said.

Just as asked, everyone remained in their seats until after Angel and Sammy, Madison and Hahna, Sienna and Little T, and Elizabeth and Olivia were at the buffet. Then they all took turns serving themselves in an orderly fashion. The food was as delicious as it smelled. And there was more than enough to feed the entire crew.

Many made desserts. Dupont showed off his culinary skills with a homemade black forest tart in a large baking dish. There were pies, brownies, and cookies including a batch that Elizabeth made, but Sammy and Hahna decorated. Those went quickly and everyone showered the two children with praise for how beautiful and delicious their cookies were.

Then they moved the tables away and moved the chairs to give everyone a great view of the Christmas Tree. They started out with the Christmas gifts from Shepherd and Diana to each of the children. Sammy and Hahna ripped open the two enormous boxes that were theirs, first.

"Oh, Mommy, Daddy, look!" Hahna exclaimed. She ran to Shepherd and Diana and first flung herself at Shepherd, giving him a hug. Then crawled onto Diana's lap and hugged her too. "Thank you!" They had gotten her a huge, three-story dollhouse with people and furniture, a dog, and a cat figure.

Sammy, taking a few minutes longer to open his, squealed in delight to find the Spiderman box of gifts containing an enormous floor puzzle, a dress up set, action figures, and Spiderman pajamas. He too ran to Shepherd and Diana to give them hugs and thank them.

Diana directed Angel, Brielle, Sienna, and Elizabeth to open the gift for their four babies at the same time.

"Oh, Diana, Shepherd, thank you," Angel said.

"Wow, that's great, thank you," Jackson seconded.

"Very cool," Doc agreed.

"Thank you so much," Elizabeth said.

"This is a great educational toy," Sienna agreed.

"Thank you. It's very generous of you,"

Garcia said.

They had gotten each of the babies a computer tablet that would grow with them. It had lights and music, would teach the alphabet, numbers, counting, and colors. It also read stories. Johanna's was pink. Olivia's was purple. The red one was for Bastian, and a blue one was for Little T.

"It will grow with them," Diana said. "You can play videos on it for them too."

Next it was time for the adults to be given their gift from the agency. Then, the remainder of the gifts were for Shepherd and Diana, one from each team, and the vast majority were for the children. They had Hahna and Sammy deliver each gift to its recipient. Only after everyone had theirs, did they open them at the same time. Shepherd flashed Angel a smile. Yes, she had outdone herself this year.

In addition to the handcrafted engraved wood signs of the couple's names that Angel picked for each couple, they also had been given a certificate for a weekend at an exclusive hotel and spa downtown overlooking Lake Michigan, including a ninety-minute couples massage and a gourmet dinner, plus a promise of the entire weekend off. The single men and Yvette were given a bottle of their drink of choice and a blank round trip airline ticket and the promise of a weekend off. Everyone thanked Shepherd. It was a generous gift.

Next, they let Sammy and Hahna open a few more gifts each from various team members. Then Shepherd and Diana opened their gift from Alpha Team. They had taken Diana and Shepherd's wedding picture, and had it made into a painted canvas which was framed beautifully.

"Oh my," Diana gushed. "It's beautiful. Thank you."

"This is a wonderful gift. Thank you," Shepherd said admiring the brush strokes.

Delta's gift was opened next. Knowing how much Shepherd and Diana liked to cook together, they'd gotten them a certificate for home gourmet in-home cooking classes, including the food for four meals to be delivered upon request. They could pick out the four meals and submit the order.

"This is great!" Diana said. "It will be so much fun to learn to make a few new dishes together."

"Thank you, this is right up our alley," Shepherd seconded.

Also knowing the couple liked wine, Charlie Team had gotten them a six-month membership in a wine club. They would receive several bottles every month. Shepherd and Diana thanked them for their thoughtful gift.

"We figured it was appropriate that we supply the booze since we probably drive you to drink," Wilson joked. The room filled with laughter.

Echo Team's gift was a four-month meat subscription delivery. From those who worked in Ops, from the Digital Team, and from Requisition Ryan, they were gifted a six-month fresh catch delivery of seafood.

"Well, it looks like you've figured us out that we like to cook, eat, and drink," Diana said.

"There's one more from just me," Michaela said. She handed the box to Hahna and had her bring it over to Shepherd and Diana.

Inside was a statue of Diana and Shepherd embracing, dressed as they had on their wedding day.

"Oh, my goodness, Michaela. It's beautiful," Diana said. Shepherd nodded as he examined it.

"My sister-in-law works in clay. I had her make it," Michaela said. "I'm sure I speak for everyone here when I say that we appreciate Shepherd Security and you, Shepherd, and we are glad that you are a part of it, Diana."

With applause, whistles, and affirming statements, everyone showed their agreement with her statement.

X-Ray

Sammy and Hahna continued to open their gifts. After, Christmas carols were sung. There was time for everyone to relax, chat, reminisce, and have a few more drinks and sample the sweet treats. It was during this time that Bravo Team caught up on the lives of their teammates who they'd worked with before being splintered off to the personal security detail they'd been on. They met their wives and girlfriends and became acquainted with them.

Angel noticed Kaylee wasn't as vibrant as usual. With Johanna on her hip, she went over to where Kaylee sat, chatting with Elizabeth. "Hi, you two," she said, pulling a chair up. "I think everything went great tonight, don't you?"

"Yes, everyone looks like they're having fun," Elizabeth said.

"Everyone but you, Kaylee. What's up?" Angel asked.

Kaylee's gaze darted to Elizabeth, and then across the room to Gary, who was talking with the men of Bravo Team. "I'm not telling anyone yet, well, I haven't, and I don't want it to be common knowledge yet, so please don't react to what I'm going to tell you, okay?"

Angel nodded, suddenly becoming worried about her friend.

"I'm pregnant," Kaylee whispered with a smile. "And I'm feeling so sick. I just went and threw up that wonderful meal."

Angel smiled and tried to school her reaction. She wanted to jump up and hug Kaylee. "Congrats," she whispered. "I have something that will help. I had horrible nausea with Johanna and Doctor Norman prescribed this for me. Let me go to my desk. I still have some."

She snuck out of the party and went to retrieve the magic formula to relieve horrendous nausea. She returned and retook her seat.

"Please don't tell anyone yet," Kaylee pleaded. "I feel like if everyone knows it will jinx it and I'll lose this one too."

"Oh, honey, it doesn't work that way," Angel said. "I promise I won't say a word. So here is what Doctor Norman had me take. He said it's perfectly safe and it's probably the same thing he'll put you on. You take half a Unisom and a B-six vitamin. If that doesn't do it, you add in one of these antinausea pills every eight hours around the clock. Don't wait until you feel sick to take it."

"Yikes, I don't know about taking meds while I'm pregnant," Kaylee said. "But if Doctor Norman prescribed it, it should be okay."

"It is. He had Michaela on it for a few months too," Angel said.

Kaylee took the three packages from Angel and immediately took one of each. "I sure hope it works. I can't be in the lavatory of the plane puking all the way to Cleveland tomorrow."

Across the room loud laughter emanated from the cluster of men who were catching up with Bravo Team. Tommy Flores was entertaining them with tales of the worst clients they protected. "And then the little shit climbed out of the window!" he said. "We were ten stories up. I don't how the hell he thought he was getting down to go back to that club."

"I think he thought he possessed the ability to rappel from balcony to balcony like you'd see in some damn video game," Elijah Robinson added. "These damn kids think they can do that shit their avatar does in games."

"Then we had the Princess as we called her," Kenny Gallup said. "This girl was sixteen going on thirty and couldn't understand why we wouldn't let her go clubbing. She had the nerve to run from me and hop on a city bus. Stupid shit didn't take into account that she was in heels and a tight skirt and I could outrun her anyway, even at my age."

The other members of Bravo Team laughed. "Ducky made her ride that bus for an hour!" Eddie Winston said laughing. "The Princess was mortified at having to ride a smelly, dirty city bus."

"Sounds like you are all glad to be done with the personal security gig," Sloan said.

They all agreed they were.

"We could have used you in Sudan," Lambchop said. "We all got some major shit done when we were in the Sandbox. I've missed working with Bravo Team. I'm glad you're back."

"We don't miss the Sandbox or any other third-world shithole, I'll tell you that," Flores said. "We've stayed at mostly five-star accommodations these past few years. We just may be a bit spoiled."

Yankee

New Year's Eve Afternoon

When Michaela pulled into the parking lot at the clubhouse in the townhouse complex where Angel and Jackson, Garcia and Sienna, and Doc and Elizabeth lived, she recognized the half-dozen cars that were already parked there. Garcia and Smith were there completing the security measures. Kaylee Sloan's car was there as expected. She had become the group's unofficial party planner, and she always did an amazing job with the decorations. Michaela had turned them over completely to her. She couldn't wait to see what Kaylee had whipped up. The only direction she gave Kaylee was that the colors turquoise and gold should be prominent.

Because there were so many people that both she and Landon were close to, the number of attendants who would stand up for them would have been ludicrous if they'd included everyone. So, they decided to exclude nearly everyone instead. Lambchop's nephew, EJ, was his best man.

Michaela's sister-in-law, Catherine, would be Michaela's matron of honor. Catherine and her niece Pippa rode with her to the clubhouse. Pippa and Hahna were her flower girls. They'd gotten the kids together to play since Gregor, Catherine, and the kids had gotten to town and the three of them played well together. Michaela's nephew, Alexander, was the same age as Hahna and Pippa was just a few years younger. He would serve as their ring bearer.

The ladies carried the garment bags their dresses were in and a small bag that contained the other items needed to dress for the wedding, which would begin in just over two hours. When Michaela stepped into the main clubhouse room she marveled at the transformation. Tears filled her eyes. Kaylee had created a beautiful, magical space.

Kaylee saw Michaela, her sister-in-law, and the little girl enter the room. Michaela's reaction was just as she'd hoped. She rushed over, all smiles. "You like it?"

"Kaylee, I love it," Michaela said.

The tablecloths were white. The flower centerpieces were a light and dark turquoise with baby's breath and greenery circled with tiny lights glowing gold atop a mirrored base that reflected the lights creating a stunning display. Strings of gold lights and turquoise and white flowers with greenery adorned the white iron arch they'd be married beneath. White lattice work sections leaned against the walls with more gold lights, greenery, and flowers in the same colors making the room feel like a garden in the middle of winter.

Kaylee embraced her. "I do too. I wasn't sure about the warm gold-colored lights with the turquoise, but it just works." Catherine's dress was gold as were Lambchop, EJ, Gregor, and Alexander's ties. Hahna and Pippa's dresses were turquoise with a wide gold ribbon that would tie like a belt.

"Thank you, Kaylee," Michaela said.

"Oh, and your flowers," she said as she drew Michaela by the hand to where several floral boxes were lined up on what would be the gift table when the guests arrived. She held up the bride's bouquet, which was in the same colors as the other flowers in the room. Gold ribbon trailed from the bouquet.

"They're beautiful," Michaela gushed, looking over not only her bouquet, but the corresponding boutonnieres for the men, the corsage for Landon's mom, the smaller bouquet for Catherine, and the two baskets of flower petals for the two flower girls to scatter.

"Landon didn't come with you?" Kaylee asked.

"No, he's up at his parent's place this

afternoon with Gregor and Alexander. They'll all come together in about an hour," Michaela said.

Garcia approached from across the room where they'd set up the onsite security post. "Hi," he greeted. "Everything is wired, and Ops is tapped in. Smith will be on in Ops with Miraldi. I'll be watching things here during the ceremony and after. Charlie Team is primary for onsite patrols, with Echo their backup. They're all due any minute. We've got everything covered."

"I never thought you wouldn't," Michaela said with a smile.

"As soon as they arrive, I'll head home to get ready. Smith's taking off now."

Michaela's gaze swept over the room. She waved at Smith. "Thank you," she called to him.

Sloan and Jackson were sliding chairs in at each table. Each chair had a turquoise ribbon tied around it with a bow at the back. Along the back wall where the buffet and bar would be, Mother and Sherman were setting the self-serve bar up.

"I'll see you and Sienna when you get back," Michaela said to Garcia. "I guess we should head to the room we're going to get ready in," she said to Catherine.

"If you need anything let me know," Kaylee said. "Gary and I are pretty much ready for the ceremony. I'll just change into my dress in the bathroom after everything out here is done."

"Thanks, Kaylee. You look beautiful just like you are. That is the cutest outfit. I thought it was what you were wearing tonight," Michaela said.

"This?" Kaylee asked glancing down at the Palazzo pants in an ocean print pattern that she had paired with a light blue silk top. "Oh, no. I have a great dress I'm wearing. It is New Year's Eve isn't it!" And she knew that if she carried this baby to term, this would be her last New Year's Eve without children. Next year, they'd have an infant and most likely would stay home for the evening.

"Yes, it is," Michaela said. She showed Catherine to the room they could get ready in. "Oh, how sweet," she remarked. Someone, probably Kaylee, had two glasses of champagne and the little bottle it was poured from and a plastic flute with a little bottle of sparkling white grape juice for Pippa. There was also a charcuterie board for them to nibble on.

Catherine lifted the two champagne glasses and handed Michaela one. "You can have a few glasses tonight. It won't hurt the baby."

***

An hour later, Lambchop and what looked like an entourage arrived in three cars. He drove his parents and his sister, Faith, in his SUV. EJ drove his two sisters in his own car. Gregor's rental car with him and Alexander pulled in behind them. Sloan met them at the door and greeted Lambchop's family. "You look beautiful this afternoon Missus J.," he said to Lambchop's mother after she released him from an embrace. "And you're looking dapper, Mister J."

"Thank you, Gary," Lambchop's mother, Nancy Johnson said.

Gary shook hands with Lambchop's father, Del, and his nephew, EJ, greeting the boy as well. He hadn't seen EJ cleaned up and dressed so nicely since EJ's mother's funeral. The girls too were all dressed up and looked beautiful. He told them as much.

Then Sloan greeted Gregor and Alexander. He'd only met Gregor once, when he accompanied Shepherd and the team that went to Greece when Michaela was in trouble. He would admit he hadn't liked Gregor much then, but he'd give him another chance tonight. He'd be friendly as Gregor didn't know many of the others from Shepherd Security and he didn't want Gregor to feel uncomfortable at his sister's wedding. From all that Lambchop had told him, Gregor had apologized for his past wrongs and was moving forward trying to make amends. That counted with Michaela and Lambchop.

Kaylee showed Gregor and Alexander to the room Michaela was in. Then Kaylee got busy distributing everyone's flowers. Doc, Elizabeth, and Olivia arrived shortly after. After Elizabeth conferred quickly with Lambchop, she too headed to the room Michaela was in. Elizabeth was excited to perform this wedding ceremony.

Zulu

The clubhouse was filled with Shepherd Security personnel and their families twenty minutes before the ceremony was due to start. The catered dinner was delivered and set up. It smelled wonderful, making everyone in the room hungry even if they'd just eaten. Battery operated flickering candles created a warm glow under the dimmed lighting in the room where soft violin music played from speakers. Michaela would have loved to have a live violinist, but as it was New Year's Eve, most were booked or had their rates so high it was ridiculous.

Lambchop had mingled for the last half hour as his teammates and their families arrived. Everyone talked about the week off they'd just enjoyed. Shepherd and Diana entered, surrounded by the men of Bravo Team as their security detail this evening.

At the top of the hour, right on schedule, Elizabeth asked everyone to take their seats. She stood at the front of the room, beneath the beautiful arch with her Bible in her hands, clutched to her chest. Olivia sat on Doc's lap but wanted Mommy. Elizabeth was afraid Olivia would cry for her during the service.

Lambchop and EJ stepped up to their places. "You'll do great," Lambchop whispered in Elizabeth's ear as he embraced her.

In the room Michaela was in, Nancy Johnson gave her a final hug. "I love you, Michaela, and I love the man you bring out in my son. Today I gain another daughter and I couldn't be happier."

"Thank you, Nancy. I love you too. You and Del raised an amazing son. I can't wait to see the father he's going to be."

Del and Nancy left the room. They would seat themselves last at a table in the front of the room with Faith and Lambchop's nieces. Everyone sat at the tables where they would eat dinner. The tables were arranged so there was an aisle Michaela would walk down, escorted by Gregor. Later, after dinner, many of the tables would be cleared to make room for dancing.

Catherine made sure the children were ready, handing the baskets of rose petals to the two little girls and explaining how to scatter them. She placed the ring pillow in Alexander's hands and reminded him how to carry it. The real rings were of course not on it.

Gregor embraced Michaela. "I love you.

Thank you for allowing me to walk you down the aisle."

"I'm glad we have a relationship, Gregor. And I'm glad you're here today."

Gregor kissed her cheek. "Mom and Dad are with us. I can feel it. They're smiling."

Tears came to Michaela's eyes. "I like that image."

Kaylee cracked open the door. "We're ready," she said with a smile. "Are you?"

Michaela laughed. "You better believe it."

Through the open door, Michaela heard the music. Kaylee directed Catherine to walk down first, which was decided would be best so the kids could follow her. Then Kaylee sent Hahna and Pippa out after her, reminding them to scatter the flower petals. When they were a few steps into the room, she sent Alexander, who ran to catch up with the girls. He wanted to throw petals too. Everyone chuckled.

Then the music changed, and Michaela and Gregor stepped into the room. Her eyes locked with Landon's at the front of the room, and he was all she saw. She had struggled to write her vows, but in that moment they became clear.

Lambchop chuckled with everyone else as Alexander ran to the girls with the ring pillow clutched under his arm like a football. He grabbed handfuls of flower petals and tossed them at the guests seated in the chairs. But then Michaela and Gregor stepped into the room and his laughter ceased. The breath left his lungs when he saw the beautiful sight in front of him. Michaela, the woman he loved. The woman he was marrying. The woman who carried his child, his daughter. She was stunning, a sight to behold.

When they reached the front of the room only then did Michaela realize everyone had stood as she came down the aisle. Gregor passed her hand to Landon and then he kissed her cheek. He took a seat in the front row beside Shepherd and Diana.

"Dearly beloved friends and family members, we gather here today to celebrate the love that Michaela and Landon share," Elizabeth began. "Today, they join their lives in the bonds of holy matrimony. It is only fitting that you, their family and friends are here to share this blessed event with them. Let us bow our heads in prayer. Lord, your servants, Michaela and Landon, come before you and these witnesses to profess their love for each other and their desire to live as husband and wife. Please bless their marriage with peace and happiness. Make their Love fruitful for Your glory and their joy, both here and in eternity. Amen."

Murmurs of "Amen," resounded through the room.

"God made Michaela and Landon for each other. They are best friends who inspire each other to be the best they personally can be. May you always support each other and applaud each other's accomplishments. May your love always foster trust and friendship between you. Marriage is a give and take and requires a dedicated effort to maintain. There will be highs and lows, sorrows and joys. May the promises you make today be lived out for the rest of your days in the life you will create together. Michaela and Landon have written their own vows." She smiled and nodded at Michaela. "Michaela will begin."

Michaela left the notes she'd made on a slip of paper, tucked away in her sleeve. She'd speak from her heart. She handed her bouquet to Catherine and then joined hands with him. "Landon, my heart recognized you as the one God had made for me, the moment I got to know you. Your kindness was the first thing that attracted me to you. Your sense of humor, intelligence, and dedication impressed me. You balance gentleness with fierceness, are the best friend anyone could ever want, and your love for your family is absolute. You serve selflessly, putting others before yourself. But what made me realize you were truly the one was the person you inspired me to be. With you in my life, I am the best person I can be.

Just because you love me, I am more trusting of everyone around me. I no longer have to keep my true self hidden away. With your love and support, I'm able to let past sorrows go. And I am able to truly trust in the Lord and accept his grace in my life. Simply put, you enhance my life in every way. I love you with all that I am. I promise to love you and cherish you all the days of my life. I promise to work every day to communicate with you openly and honestly and to put our life together, and our family, ahead of anything else. I promise to always be your best friend."

Tears streaked down her face and unshed tears were in his eyes as well.

"Landon," Elizabeth prompted.

"Michaela, like many of my brothers on the team, I have seen the worst of life. I have seen death and accepted long ago that my mortal life could end whenever God decided to call me home. Everyone knows that it was in those times that I came to know God and dedicated my life to His work. But in your eyes, through your smiles, and from your loving embraces, I have seen the best my future could hold. The first time I met you, long ago, I was captivated by the beautiful person you are, inside and out. I immediately saw a soul that overflowed with kindness and love. I saw an intelligence that impressed me and drew me in, needing to know more about you. Friendship was all we were allowed to share because of our jobs. I accepted that but always wanted more because I too, knew that you were the one God had made for me. But I had faith that in His perfect time, He would enable us to be together. And while we waited, our friendship deepened. You accept me for who I am, Michaela, which is a gift. You love me with all your heart, and I feel it every day. I love you and promise to always be worthy of your love. I promise to love, honor, and cherish you all the days of our lives. I promise to always be faithful to you. I promise to always be your best friend."

"Michaela and Landon have said their vows. They have chosen to exchange rings, the outward symbol of those vows and commitment to each other. Throughout time, the wedding ring has also signified never-ending love, a circle of completeness. It has no beginning and no end, just as your love for one another." She removed Landon's ring from her thumb and handed it to Michaela. "Michaela, repeat after me."

Michaela held the ring at the tip of his ring finger of his left hand.

"I give you this ring. Wear it with love and joy."

Michaela repeated the words.

"As this ring has no end, my love is also forever."

Michaela repeated the words, her voice becoming shakier with emotion as she spoke. She slid the plain gold band onto Landon's finger.

Then Elizabeth took the ring for Michaela from her finger and handed it to him. "Landon, repeat after me."

He recited the same words as he slid the beautiful, diamond circled band onto Michaela's finger.

"May rings you exchanged today always remind you that you are surrounded by enduring love. By the authority vested in me, I now pronounce you husband and wife. What God has put together let no one separate. Landon, you may kiss your wife."

He wrapped his arms around her and drew her against himself for their first kiss as husband and wife. Their friends and family cheered. They were both breathless when they ended the kiss.

"For the first time, I introduce Mister and Missus Landon Johnson," Elizabeth proclaimed.

There was more applause, whistles, and hollers.

"I love you Missus Johnson," he said to her.

Her eyes were locked on his. She saw the love in them. "I love you too, my husband."

EJ slapped Lambchop on the shoulder.

Lambchop turned to face him and saw that he had tears in his eyes. EJ fiercely embraced him. "Congrats!"

Lambchop and Michaela embraced Elizabeth. "That was an amazing ceremony!" he said to her.

They were then congratulated and embraced by their friends and family after that, as everyone stood and took turns approaching the couple. The room was loud until Michaela and Landon took their seats at their table. Kaylee started tapping her fork against a water goblet, and the others joined in, the noise in the room quieting. Michaela and Landon stood and kissed to applause.

"We both want to thank you all for coming," Lambchop said. "The bar is open if you haven't gotten a drink yet, please do."

Many raised their glasses into the air as if to say, already have.

"The food smells amazing, and just like on Christmas Eve, let's let the families with children go first. I know it's traditionally supposed to be the wedding couple, but Michaela and I will go after them. Getting the children's plates can take a little more time."

After everyone had filled their plate and were seated at the table, EJ stood. "As best man, I'm told I'm supposed to give the first toast. I've never done this before, so cut me some slack if it's not like it's supposed to be. I was told to speak from my heart, so here goes. To my Uncle L and Michaela. Uncle L, you have always been the best role model for me and my sisters. You've always been there for us, the dad we never had. You've taught me about honor and what it means to be a man. And Michaela, when our mother died, you were there to hold our hands and offer your support. You didn't try to replace our mom, but you were there to help us as she would have wanted. The two of you together show us what love is supposed to look like, just like what we see with Grandma and Grandpa. I wish you a lifetime of love and happiness. Your baby is one lucky kid! To Uncle L and Michaela!" He cried as he spoke. Lambchop embraced him when he was through speaking.

Not a single woman in the room had a dry eye. His toast affected all of them. Many of the men had moisture in their eyes as well. Many more toasts followed as everyone ate. Immediately after dinner they cut the cake. Kaylee, Annaka, and Madison plated it and set them on a table for anyone to grab a piece as Sloan, Mother, Jackson, and Cooper cleared a few of the tables and moved the chairs to create a dance floor.

Once again, Sherman's brother Bobby acted as DJ, just as he did at Shepherd and Diana's wedding. He called them to the floor for their first dance as a married couple. They chose *Thank God* by Kane and Katelyn Brown. Half-way through the song, Bobby invited all their guests to join. Cooper held Hahna in his arms and Madison came in close embracing them both in a Cooper family group hug. The three of them danced. Brielle and Sherman did the same with their son, Bastian, as did Sienna and Garcia with Little T nestled between them. Jackson danced with Johanna and right in front of him, snuggled in close, Angel held Sammy in her arms. Doc and Elizabeth also held Olivia between them as they danced.

Sloan held Kaylee close as they swayed with the music. He nodded at Sienna, Garcia, and Little T beside them. "That will be us at the next wedding," he whispered.

They'd been to the OB a few days earlier. The pregnancy looked healthy. The anti-nausea concoction Angel had given Kaylee on Christmas Eve had worked, and Doctor Norman prescribed it for Kaylee as well.

By twenty-two hundred, ten p.m., those with children were saying their good nights to everyone and congratulating Michaela and Lambchop one last time. They were heading home to get their little ones to bed. Doc and Elizabeth took Hahna with them so Madison and Cooper could stay and celebrate the New Year. Joe Lassiter took his leave then as well.

The party lasted late into the night, with a countdown at midnight and the traditional singing of Auld Lang Syne. Shepherd and Diana left shortly after, again shadowed by Bravo Team. Continuing with his usual gift, Shepherd had given the couple their honeymoon trip. They would fly out the next morning for Hawaii to spend a week there, wishing to revisit where they'd first become a couple.

In their home in the nearby townhouse community, Jackson tucked Sammy in bed as Angel nursed Johanna for the final time that night in the nursery down the hall. He read Sammy a story, surprised he was still awake. They thought for sure Sammy would have fallen asleep in the car on the way home.

He rocked Sammy in the padded rocking chair in the corner of the room to try to help settle the wide-awake preschooler. As he snuggled with his son, tears came to his eyes recalling the evening. Whenever one of the team, one of his brothers were married, he'd always reflect on the moment that Angel walked down the aisle. And of course, he was then filled with the feelings he had when he first realized that he'd fallen in love with her and would have given up his entire life to be with her. Visions of nearly losing her still flashed into his thoughts on occasion, not that he'd admit that to Dr. Lassiter. And of course, he couldn't help but remember the day when she'd healed from her trauma, and they'd made love again. His heart soared knowing the happiness and full life he had, a life he never thought was possible.

He kissed the top of Sammy's head, his son, a product of his and Angel's love. He wasn't sure what he'd done to deserve this wonderful family he had, and he prayed they'd never be taken from him. That thought scared the shit out of him. He was happy Lambchop had found that with Michaela. EJ had been correct when he said, their baby would be one lucky kid.

In just two days, he would be back to work, back to reality. The week off had been a welcomed respite, his family wrapping him in a cocoon of calmness and normalcy. But evil and danger still lurked and until he deemed the world to be a safe enough place for Sammy and Johanna to grow up in, he'd continue to do the job. Besides, he still felt fulfilled doing it.

He was so deep in thought that he hadn't noticed that Sammy slept or that Angel entered until she was beside him. She leaned over and kissed his lips. He wiped a stray tear that had dripped onto his cheek. He never had to be ashamed of crying in front of Angel. She understood and she knew him better than he knew himself most of the time.

"He's asleep," she whispered. She took Sammy from his arms and placed him in bed. She kissed his forehead and tucked the covers in. Then she went back to the chair and extended a hand to Jackson.

He rose and left the room with her. But instead of immediately going to their room, he crept into Johanna's room and watched her sleep for a few minutes. He kissed the tips of his fingers and gently placed them on her tiny sleeping form.

When he entered their bedroom, Angel had already changed into her flannel nightgown. He went to her and kissed her before he pulled it over her head. "You are more beautiful than the first time I saw you naked in my room at the Silo." He glanced at his watch. It was nearly twenty-three hundred hours. "What do you say, Missus Jackson, shall we spend the next hour naked and ring in the New Year with our own fireworks?"

"Ah, I see a new Holiday Tradition taking hold," she said with a lustful grin. She reached out and unbuttoned his shirt. She slid it from his shoulders. His muscled physique still drew her eyes to wander over his body. Then she undid his pants and pushed them and his boxer briefs down his legs. His member sprung to attention and saluted her. She kissed his lips. "There, that's much better. You were overdressed."

"I love you, my Angel."

"And I love you with all my heart. Happy

New Year, my darling."

The End

The Shepherd Security Series

Book 1: Operation Protected Angel

Book 2: Operation Recruited Angel

Book 3: Operation Dark Angel

Book 4: Operation Fallen Angel

Book 5: Operation Departed Angel

Book 6: Operation Bayou Angel

Book 7: Operation Unknown Angel

Book 8: Operation Beach Angel

Book 9: Operation Healing Angel

Book 10: Operation Trusted Angel

Book 11: Operation Spirit Angel

Book 12: Operation Blood Angel

Book 13: Operation Shadow Angel

Book 14: Operation Reluctant Angel

Book 14.5: A Shepherd Security Christmas

Book 15: Operation Reckless Angel – Coming January 2024

There are 9 more book planned in The

Shepherd Security Series

Also by Margaret Kay

That First Year - A story of love, loss, family, and resiliency, with hope, tears, and laughter.

A women's contemporary Romance, family life fiction story of a fifty-year-old woman and her three adult children and their lives during That First Year following the death of her husband/their father.

Please stay in touch. I love to hear from readers! And remember to check out my sister's books. You can be kept abreast of my sister's work and mine at our website:

Visit our website at: www.sistersromance.com

Email me at: MargaretKay@sistersromance.com

Follow me on Facebook at: https://www.facebook.com/MargaretKayAuthor

Subscribe to the Sisters Romance Newsletter to be kept informed of when my next books are due out at:

Subscribe to our Newsletter

Acknowledgements

I truly say thank you, to you, the reader, for choosing this book. If you enjoyed it, would you please leave a review, so others might find this book to enjoy, as well? As an Independent Author, without a publishing house to help advertise my work, I rely on reviews from readers such as you and followers on social media to promote me. Thank you! I would greatly appreciate it.

Thank you to my sisters, RK Cary and Charlie Roberts, who are writing their own Romance books. RK has finished up her Destined & Redeemed series and has several other Science Fiction/Fantasy stories in the works. Charlie is working on a contemporary romance series, the Stevens Street Gym Series. Both have been wonderful friends with the honesty and encouragement that only a sister can give. Check out their work on Amazon! Links directly to all our books on Amazon can be found on our website. The link is below.

Thank you to my wonderful and supportive husband for his patience and love while I spend hours upon hours to research and write this story. Also, for advising me on any parts of this story requiring knowledge of the military or weapons that I did not have.

Thank you to my mother who shared with me her love of books. As a child, the wonderful example my mother set for me as an avid reader led my sisters and me to write our stories. She has encouraged me to publish, and I thank her for her support.

Thank you to my two adult children, Steve and Rachel. You have both given me wonderful support and I hope I have made you proud!

My friend, photographer, and graphic artist, Harry R., photographed and created all the covers for this series. Thank you, Harry!

A big thank you to my girlfriends who have encouraged me and made me feel that I could do this at the times I felt insecure in my ability to accomplish this. You know who you are ladies! You hold a special place in my heart.

Thank you to my editors, a special callout to Evelin, who gave of her time selflessly to help me with the grammar, not my strongpoint. And thank you to my ARC Team.

About the Author

Hello! I am Margaret Kay. I am a wife to my best friend of thirty-nine years, a mother of two adult children, a grandmother, and a dog-mom who makes my own dog food. I have been fortunate that I have been able to turn my passion of daydreaming about characters and storylines into books that people want to read.

They say being a Military wife is the toughest job in the Armed Forces even though there is no MOS for the position. As the veteran of more than a few deployments, I must agree. My husband proudly served eight years in the United States Navy in the 80s. That was before cell phones and the internet.

For anyone who's never had a loved one who's served, being associated with the military is being part of a special community of people who support each other, who understand what the day to day is like when your loved one is deployed half-way around the world.

Saying goodbye to your loved one as they

leave on a lengthy deployment is unlike saying goodbye to someone for any other reason. It's not like dropping a son or daughter at college or hugging an aging parent after a visit. Your military member is being deployed, part of a mission. You cannot go visit when you miss them too much. You know it's different. You plan for it differently. They may be getting deployed into harm's way. And even if they are not, you know what their purpose is and that they could be in harm's way at any time.

The emotions you feel when you stand with other families, when the unit, boat, or flight returns after many months of separation cannot be described in words that bring adequate justice to it, but I will try. There is a level of excitement equaled only by a child's wonder on Christmas morning. A pride in your country, in the unit, and in your loved one that surges through your vein's as you, your children, and all around you hold American flags and signs welcoming them home, waiting all together sometimes for hours before they appear and make their way towards you. As a spouse, you're hungering for your partner's touch, for their lips to meet yours, and for the reunion that will occur later, when you're alone. With that excitement also comes nervousness because it has been so long since you've been together as a couple, sharing your bed.

My husband honorably separated from the Navy and easily transitioned to civilian life, but

I never forgot what it was like while he served. Many of our returning servicemen and women have not had it so easy. Please keep them in your thoughts and prayers as they recover from physical and emotional injuries. Many struggle to find employment. If you have the ability in your work to encourage the hiring of a Vet, please do.

Our military members are special! I honor all past, present, and future members of our military with my stories. Salute the flag, stand for the national anthem, and thank a Vet for their service. Freedom is not free; a lot of people have sacrificed for the freedoms we enjoy.

Don't ever forget!

Margaret

www.ingramcontent.com/pod-product-compliance
Lightning Source LLC
Chambersburg PA
CBHW030335180626
46810CB00003B/1363